MANGLED
MEAT

EDWARD LEE

deadite
press

DEADITE PRESS
205 NE BRYANT
PORTLAND, OR 97211

AN ERASERHEAD PRESS COMPANY
WWW.ERASERHEADPRESS.COM

ISBN: 1-936383-78-0

CONTENTS

THE DECORTICATION
TECHNICIAN

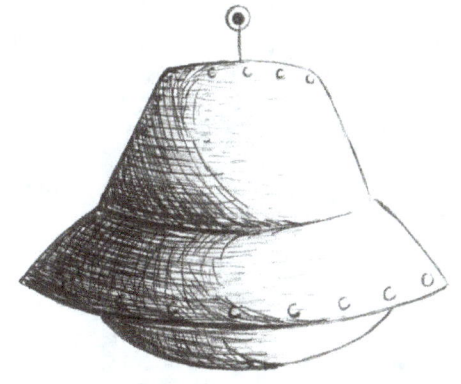

You ever shit your pants? I did a couple of days ago, first time in my life, but, see, at the time I wasn't wearing just pants, I was wearing a pair of sealed Class III EUDs. That's plat-talk for environmental utility dress—a spacesuit, to creamcake earth-loving non-hackers like you.

The recovery platoon brought it in at about 0300 zulu, *it* clearly being a hyper-velotic vehicle of extraterrestrial origin. Heel-shaped, twenty meters long, thirty wide. A dull-gray finish just like the old "UFO" fables from a quarter of a millennium ago. No viewports, no passive vid-lenses—no windows of any kind.

No doors.

Obviously this space-canoe came from a technology far superior to the Federated World's. Since I was the plat's decort tech, the OAC ordered me to assist in the r-dock, and, no, that's not when I shit my pants. I was jazzed just like the rest of the crew. This was the find of all of human history, and we were part of it. We'd all be famous. Our names would be in the history chips for as long as humankind endured, and with successful colonies on fifty-seven planets now, it's a good bet that humankind will endure for quite a while.

I open things, that's my job. I open things very carefully. That's why the OAC ordered me to the dock and no one else. Lotta sour grapes there, I can tell you, but to hell with 'em. When the OAC talks, you jump. Once the grunts brought this thing into the retrieval dock, we scanned it every which way but couldn't find any seams, no sign of any kind of entrance. We could only presume it was pressurized but God knew with what, so that ruled out a hot cut. And another thing: when we p/a/a'd the hull, it told us it was made of a non-metallic element as yet undiscovered.

"Burn the fucker open," SSG Yung said. "*Blow* it open with some C-11."

"Yeah, yeah!" the rest of his bohunkers shouted.

Just like ground-pounders, I thought. "Have you boys been drinking the cooling-tube effluvium again? Any gas inside the craft could be flammable. We could blow up the whole plat, you mallet-heads."

"Well then how are we gonna open it?" Yung grumbled. "We *gotta* open it!"

"Yeah, yeah!" the rest of his platoon shouted.

"We don't *gotta* do anything of the sort," I told the idiots. "We don't know anything about it. We start fucking around with it, we could destroy it—and ourselves. Smartest thing to do is secure it in one of the hold-warrens. Take it back to earth when the mission's done."

"That's three years!" Yung bellowed. "We got a fuckin' *alien spaceship* here, and there might be a fuckin' *alien* inside. We're supposed to wait three fuckin' years before we find out what's fuckin' inside the motherfucker?"

"You speak with the eloquence of kings," I remarked, but then, just as I'd voiced my objection, the OAC appeared on my head's-up-display.

:-cE jONSIN, dT1163: aTTEMPT tO eNTER tHE oBJECT-:

"Yeah, yeah!" Yung and his whitewalls shouted.

Orders were orders, so that was it. "You guys got what you wanted. Evacuate the r-dock."

"No way," Yung took some exception. "We busted our balls hauling this tin can aboard. We're damn sure gonna be here when you open it."

I shook my head. "It's for your own safety. You guys gotta leave."

Six grinning meat-racks in EUDs surrounded me.

"*Make* us leave, civvie."

"Suit yourself," I said, getting the point. "Prep me. I want this victor covered with lexlar blast blankets. Keep the dock de-preshed. And charge me up a nute-drill and a quarter-inch blackie-pete bit..."

I guess I should back up a little, huh? Set things off right? I mean, I got no idea when this log-chip might be found, and I guess it's highly probably whoever finds it won't know what the hell this is all about.

My name's Dug Jonsin, twenty-nine earth years old. Mission ID: DT1163. It's Tuesday, 25 May 2202. I'm a civilian astro-entomologist attached to the Federated World's Academy of Galactic Studies. I examine and catalogue insects by academic design, but what I really do is cut them open. Officially, I'm a FOS 95C20 Decortication Technician.

Sounds fancy but...I'm a light-weight by earth standards. My college GPA was only 3.89. Couldn't get a good job with the Academy earthbound, so here I am on this tub which they call a Deep Space Analytic and Collection Platform, vessel tag CW-DSP-141. Fourteen-man crew: six Army grunts for the retrieval platoon, one Jarine security ape who doubles as a corpsman, two more civvies like me on the Technistics Unit, and five Naval Space Corp dupes who run the plat.

And me.

The job's a cake walk, really. We hit different star clusters, ID planets, planetoids, moons, and asters with nitrogen-oxygen atmospheres, and then we check them out. Fauna and flora, for the Academy's zoological indexes. The FW's been running survey missions like this for over a hundred years, since the invention of I-grav drives. That's inverted-gravity propulsion. A simple cadmium laser electrically charges a Palladium/Peridotite ceramic plate and harnesses one-half of available interspacial gravity as a force of propulsion. The lasers provide specific photon wavelengths to pass or dissipate the electrical charge through a gallium isolator. Cadmium for ON, Helium for OFF. Simple. It proved that the Twentieth Century eggheads were right. You can't beat the speed of light, but you can sure as shit bend it. That's how we can move our platforms far out of the Milky Way. So much for universal invariants.

Each mission is a ten-year gig, but they say you only age about three and a half. Nobody wants this shit so there's a pay off. Early retirement on the fed lamb. I figured it was worth it. No wife, no kids—could never afford that stuff. But when I get back to earth I can have it all. Phenothiazines keep you from going insane, and tetra-amine implants kill your sex drive. A lot of the crew don't believe it at first, so they sneak on porn chips, but after the implant, man, you can look at a holopegs of Miss Defense Corp buck naked but it's about as erotic as looking at your own turds in a gravity toilet. I haven't had a hard-on in seven years, wouldn't know what to do with it if I did. Every month the OAC orders you to sit on a rectal bolus; a sub-static charge that makes you ejaculate so you don't get prostate cancer down the road.

Oh, and the OAC? That stands for Operational Analysis Computer. There's no captain on this rowboat, just the OAC. When it gives you an order, you do it. If you don't, you get cryo'd, and when you get back to the World, you get no compensation, no retirement, no nothing. Just ten years of your life down the drain and sometimes a full nickel stint on the Lunar Detention Facility.

So if this crap-pot full of microchips tells me to stand on my head and cluck like a chicken, I don't ask why, I just do it.

But back to my FOS—that's Federal Occupational specialty. Astro-entomolgy is the fancy way of putting it, bug-cracking is the more realistic way. I'm a decorticator. One thing we found out fast after we started searching other solar systems for signs of life is that there were *all kinds* of life on a lot of these rocks.

Just nothing interesting.

Nothing mammalian. Usually just microscopic stuff like entozoas, chlorophiles, trimeciums—space germs—and we'd cryo the samples and that was it. Same thing with vegetation, thallophytes, and fungus. Tag it and freeze it.

But another thing we found a lot of were what could be categorized in earth terms as *insectas*: hexapods, anthropods—aquatic and terrestrial—anything with an exoskeleton. And a lot of them were pretty big.

Ever seen a cockroach the size of a 55-gallon drum? Ever seen a moth the size of a bald eagle? We'd get so much stuff like that—alien insecta phylas—that you wouldn't believe it. For an entomologist, it was exciting as hell.

For about a month.

Then it all got to be the same. When the exploratory surveys started, there was this idealistic hope that someday one of the missions would find mammalian life, would even find something akin to the human species. But that never happened.

All we found were bugs.

Big bugs. Insects that had evolved for millions or even billions of years and had genetically adapted a physical size that could accommodate longevity. Heavily shelled creatures that could withstand hostile environments, drastic fluctuations in atmospheric pressure and content, neutrino and meteoric showers and volcanic debris.

Big bugs. Big bugs with hard shells. That's pretty much what the rest of the galaxy had waiting for mankind to discover.

So that was my job.

As the mission's decortication tech, I had to take two samples of each sex of any insecta we discovered. One sample I'd cryo immediately. The other sample I'd autopsy if the creature's size was deemed by the OAC as practical. Some of these things had three of four sexes. And a lot of them were huge.

I had to establish the most effective way to decorticate the insect while still alive. In other words, I had to cut off its hull, shell, carapace, exoskeleton, or whatever, and autopsy the bug while digigraphing the entire procedure for the Academy's archives.

Yeah, yeah, I know what you're thinking. How hard can it be to cut the shell off a bug?

Space bugs? It's a bitch. See, I gotta do it without destroying the bug. You don't use scissors. You don't use a knife—not for this job. You don't pin the goddamn thing to a board. Some of these things are as big a man, bigger. If you try to open 'em with an ectine torch, all you'll do it fry the damn thing. And if you fry it, the OAC logs that into your service file as a demerit.

You should see some of the shit that these bugs got inside of them. Black slop, brown slop, green slop. Slimy organs whose purpose you couldn't even guess at. Hell, one time I decorticated an octopod from P31 on the Ryan Cluster—I cut the sheath off the groinal trap and this thing had something that looked just like a human cock! No lie! This thing didn't have an ovidpositur—it had a dick!

So, anyway, that's my ten-year gig. Decorticating bugs.

11

I never would've imagined that, one day, I'd be ordered to decorticate something else.

It was the MADAM that picked it up first—that's Mass-Activated-Detection-Alarm-Mechanism. It's a souped-up spheric-pulse radar, picks up anything in the scan field that the OAC calculates can't be organically or naturally formed.

We'd just hypervelled through the Zuby System, using grids piped to us from the Hubble 6 matrix, and we weren't thrusting through this white-dwarf system for more than an hour before the MADAM went off. The OAC called General Quarters, and all we could do then was wait. Wait for the tri-wave scans to bounce back to the sensor-slats and tell us what was out there.

The OAC told us this:

:-mADAM cOORDINATES vIA hOME pLATFORM aS zERO: sEVEN-sIX-tHREE dEGREES sIX mINUTES oN mENISCUS cHART. pROBABLITY cOMPUTATIONS iNDICATE nINE-nINE-pERCENT lIKELIHOOD oF eXTRATERRESTRIAL vEHICLE oF hIGHER tECHNOLOGY dERIVATION tHAN iS pREVIOUSLY iNDEXED-:

I'd been sitting in the chow hall, eating gengineered monkfish-steak when that call came through. The Army grunts were scrambled, and thrusted out on a retrieval skiff in less time that than it takes to fill your piss bag. About an hour later, they were redocking and asking for ingress countercodes. The OAC passed them through, and that's when I was ordered to r-dock.

You're still wondering what this has to do with me shitting my EUDs, right? Well, I'm getting to that. I'm standing on the lock-rails in r-dock when the grunts bring the victor in and tack it down to the stulls. They close the dock door but wisely don't represh; we all keep our CVC helmets on with defoggers set on high. This victor—vehicle—looked stunning, a perfect crescent with no seams, no doors, no visual outlets or propulsion vents, no indiction even of a gravity-amplification node.

Just a thirty-meter-wide crescent, a giant boomerang.

The laze scales put the thing in at just under two-hundred pounds. Something that big? It should've weighed at least a couple of tons. Which meant that whatever unknown element it was made of had very little weight, very little photon mass. It was at the least a kick to have the grunts following my orders. Federal Military didn't like it when civilians told them what to do. But I was the expert here, at least the best that this mission could provide. My expertise involved cutting bugs open. Therefore I was the best candidate to cut open an alien vehicle.

"Pop this can," one of the field privates muttered, wide-eyed behind his glexan visor. "Crack it open."

"Do it," SSG Yung said.

"What do you think I'm going to do? Play paddycakes with it?" I strapped on the force harness, then closed the chuck on the Black & Decker neutron drill; the treated black-phosphorus bit would make a million-and-a-half cycles per minute but it wouldn't get hot. No heat conduction, no sparks. "And if this doesn't work, I'll try the nuclear spanner." I raised the massive drill on its waist-bracket, then planted my nanoboots on the floorwall and pressed the bit against the victor's hull.

"Hardcore," someone said.

"Last chance to evac, guys," I reminded them. I winked at SSG Yung.

"Just rev that fuckin' thing up and go!" Yung yelled.

Suit yourself. I toggled down the charge lever, flipped open the safety. Just as I was about to hit the power detent—

"Wait a minute!" a platoon Spec 4 shouted. He was standing on the other side of the victor, running a hand-held photon-activation-analysis scan on the hull.

"What?" I said, the drill harness weighing down on my hips.

"You ain't gonna believe this...but I've got double-pozz poroscopy on the hull, and residual chloride ions."

"*Bull*shit!" I practically spat into my mic.

"I shit you not, man," the Spec replied. "Ain't nothing else this could be."

It's got to be a mistake, I thought, but I unstrapped the drill anyway.

"What the fuck are you fuckin' talkin' about?" Yung complained. "Chloride *what?*'

"Chloride *ions,*" I said. "It's part of a typical sebaceous amino acid secretion, unless that OAC's glitching. Your man just found a *fingerprint* on the hull."

Yung's eyes opened as wide as a condenser slug behind his visor. "The *fuck?*"

"It looks overlayed a bunch'a times," the Spec 4 observed, focusing the p/a/a screen. I checked it out myself and he was right.

"No ridge patterns," I said more to myself than to him. "The pore pattern's relatively intact, but that's it. Then it looks like..."

"A smear?" the Spec ventured.

"Yeah, I think so. Digigraph it a couple of times and save the files in the OAC," I said. Then I turned to SSG Yung, who still didn't get it.

"Someone or some thing touched this victor, Sergeant Yung. And whoever touched it, touched it repeatedly in the same place."

Behind the glex visor, Yung's face twisted up. "You mean a *human?*"

"Well, something clearly human*oid,*" I corrected. "Something that has sebaceous secretions similar to ours."

"All right...uh— Just get back on that drill and cut this fucker open," he said.

Be as dumb as you can be—in the Army, I thought. "The nute-drill could take hours or days. Let me try something. If it doesn't work, then I'll power the drill back up. Is that square with you?"

Yung smirked, reached up and tried to scratch his chin before he remembered he was wearing a sealed CVC. "Yeah, fuck, all right."

"Represh the dock to six-five," I told the Spec. Yung nodded consent. It took a few minutes but I needed enough PSIs in the dock to take my EUD mitt off. Then I grabbed an

SV probe off the hardware lock.

"What the fuck are you fuckin' doin'?" Yung asked.

I didn't bother answering. The sub-violet lume element would show me the same spot where the hull was touched. "There it is," I muttered. It was a downward streak. Someone had pressed his or her fingertip against the hull at this precise point. Then they'd dragged their fingertip down in a straight line...

With my mitt off, then, I did the same thing. I pressed my fingertip on the same spot, then dragged it down.

A small ingression on the high quadrant of the hull formed. And for you earth-loving no-hackers who don't know what that means... It means a doorway opened.

"He did it!" Yung barked. "The candyass civvie fuck *did* it! First Platoon! Lock and load." Yung shoved me back out of the way as his troops charged their Colt M-57 Squad Assault Systems. "Cole, Alvirez, take firing positions at the bulkhead! Filips and Bensin, cover the entrance at one-five meters! Come on, Roburts! It's me and you."

"Sarge, Sarge," I interrupted. "The G.I. Joe stuff isn't going to be necessary." I showed him my fileflat which was now out-indexing the atomic chromatography specs from the p/a/a scan. "Check this out."

Yung frowned at the readouts, his trigger finger twitching. "The fuck am I supposed to know what that shit is? I ain't no wirehead—I'm a fuckin' Army Ranger!"

Tell me about it. "This is a radio assay and carbon-date of the fingerprint. It's over 2,000 years old, Sarge. Any life form inside that victor is long dead."

"Balls," the platoon sergeant replied. "Cover me, Roburts!" Then he raised his weapon and entered the craft. I guess these guys had their games to play, so what the hell. They had to go through the motions, I guess to maintain their identities. And I guess I did the same thing, in my own way, too.

But when Yung entered the victor with his wrist-light and rifle—it seemed like a whole lot of time went by with all of us just standing there staring at the doorway. Yung didn't respond. We couldn't even see his shadow moving in there.

"Hey, Sarge?" I called out.

Nothing.

"Sergeant Yung! Relay your status!" one of the other grunts cracked.

Nothing.

Then—

"Holy everlovin' motherfuckin' shit..."

It was Yung's voice that carried back to our CVCs. I turned to the SGT E-5 next to me. "You're next in command, pal. You better send someone in there."

"I-I-I—," he stammered.

What the hell, I thought. I grabbed the SGT's wrist-light and stepped into the victor. The cabin walls were black but somehow tinged with silver. I saw no evidence of an operator's seat, instruments, or controls. Just the weird silver-black, which sucked up the 1000-candle-power sodium light I was carrying.

"Down here," Yung's voice drifted to me.

It was like walking through black fog. I seemed to take many more steps than the depth of the craft would allow, but eventually Yung's form came into focus. He'd dropped his weapon on the victor's floor and was just sitting there on a starboard protrudement.

"Guess I just wasn't ready for it," he said. He sat there with the rim of his helmet in his palm. He looked out of it. He looked whacked.

"What's that, Sarge?"

"Seen a lot of fucked up shit in my time. Seen guys die, my own men, seen whole transport plats blow up 'cos some mech jockey forgot to close a vent-line. I saw the P-4 quake split the whole planetoid in half and swallow fifteen thousand colonists five minutes after my thruster took off. It's fucked up shit, man."

"Straighten up, Sarge," I said. For whatever reason, he was going down memory lane, and the scenery wasn't too great. "Get yourself squared away. Sure, we're standing inside an alien spacecraft—the first one ever discovered—and you're right, it's fucked up. But we gotta keep it together. We got our jobs to do. You got men out there shit-scared. They're counting on you."

His CVC turned toward me. Through the glex visor, I could see his blank eyes in the light. "Since I was a little kid," he droned, "I always thought that this would happen someday. But it was just a fantasy, you know? Some kids fantasize about being president, some kids fantasize about seeing an alien.... Man, this is fucked up."

The tone of his words wrapped me up. "Seeing...a what?" I said. But now I guessed his point. We knew there must have been something inside this ship, however long dead. What else could it be but an "alien?" A "spaceman?" Something every man, woman, and child in the Federate had thought about, dreamed about, but something, by now, that nobody really believed in anymore. Like afterlife, reincarnation, spirituality. Just myths now. Mankind in the 23rd century no more believed in spacemen than they believe in Santa Claus.

Yung's voice cracked like tinder. "Take a look, civvie," he said.

I let my light follow his gaze. Some kind of a molded object rose from the floor, something like a chair, and sitting in that chair was the victor's obvious pilot.

An ecstatic chaos filled the plat, everyone running around like meth-freaks. Time seemed to stand still. The OAC ordered most of the crew to analyze the victor. As for the dead pilot, of course we couldn't analyze *him* until we got his suit off. That was my job: to decorticate the pilot, so to speak. To remove his environmental suit and extract the body for digigraphics and autopsy.

We'd moved the body to the medcove, lain it out on an exam table under the lumes.

"Twenty-one May, 2202," I said into the mission recorder. "Jonsin, Dugliss, FOS 95C20 decortication technician for mission survey on DSP-141. The Operational Analysis Computer has ordered me to attempt to extract the body of the victor's apparent operator for analysis and archives indexing.

For this record, the victor's operator will be referred to as VO from here on..."

Oh, damn. Some story teller I am, huh? I forgot to tell you what the guy looked like. Humanoid and bipedal. Two pronating arms, two pronating legs, and a head. Each hand showing four fingers with three phalanges, and an opposable thumb. One hundred and forty-six point four pounds via specific earth gravity, and seventy-one inches long in extremis. For all intents, it was a guy in a spacesuit with a general surface anatomy similar to ours.

But it was still an alien, and it was the ev-suit that kept reminding me of that. Same color, same hue as the ship: a flat silver-black. To the touch, the material felt like something polycron or cloth, but if you pressed down on it, it wouldn't give at all. I tried a particle vise on the right thumb and *nothing happened.* The vise broke at 750,000 psi. But if you grabbed the hand, you could bend the fingers in their natural direction. Same with the rest of the body. The suit was pliable...but then again, it wasn't.

The head was the weirdest part. Not a helmet, nothing like what you would think of as utility headgear. Just a bullet-shape extending from the shoulders. No visor, no visual ports, no bumps where the ears should be. Just imagine dipping a doll in wax enough times that only the basic shape remained.

This was my company for about the next seventy-two hours. First thing I tried was a standard scan of the suit, same way I'd scan a bug before cutting it open. But this was no bug. X-rays, V-rays, triax tomography, nuclear-resonance scans—all negative. And it was no big surprise that, like the victor, the VO's suit showed no signs of any sort of opening. No zipper on this spaceman. And I tried touching the suit, like I'd touched the ship, but...no such luck.

The only way to see what was inside was to do what I did best. Cut it open.

I didn't sleep for days; I only ate when the OAC ordered me to. I became obsessed, but then everyone else was too—*obsessed* with their particular mission assignments. This was history, this was *it*. And we were all a working part.

But for *my* part—failure.

Section lasers, nuke-picks, impact-bezels, the sub-cabundum band-saw, the ectine torch? All of them failed. Whatever material it was that the VO's suit was constructed of, none of these tools touched it. I couldn't dent it, couldn't melt it, couldn't even scratch it. Detcord failed too, and so did beta-fluoric acid. Nothing. The most invasive and corrosive substances and tools known to man did *nothing* to the VO's suit.

In the meantime, though, I learned from the OAC updates that the rest of the crew were having the same bad luck trying to take the victor apart. Every single testing and analysis method available could determine absolutely nothing about the composition, structure, or engineering of the craft. And since no propulsion system could be detected, God knew how this thing got to the Zuby system. Where was it coming from? Where was it going?

Eventually, though, a half-answer blipped over our HUDs. Since no engine, fuel, or propulsion structures were discovered on the victor, the OAC, after almost three earth days of computations half a trillion cycles per second, told us this:

:-cALCULATIONS fOUNDED iN aLL kNOWN qUANTUM pOSTULATION eSTIMATES tHAT fOREIGN vICTOR mAY bE pROPELLED bY sOME dESIGN oF rELATIVISTIC mOMENTUM-eNERGY rELATION bASED oN pRPOSED 20th-cENTURY tHEORY. $E = pc$ aND mo [momentum] = 0. iF a pHOTON cEASES tO mOVE aT tHE sPEED oF lIGHT, iT cEASES tO eXIST. tHEREFORE, tHERE iS a hIGH pROBABLILITY tHAT tHE vICTOR iS pROPELLED bY pHOTONIC wAVELENGTH eQUALIZATION. hIGH bERYLLIUM vAPOR-pHASE tHROUGH tRACKED pROXIMITY oF zUBY sTAR sYSTEM wOULD dISABLE sUCH a pOWERPLANT-:

So there is was. The most off-the-wall theory of motion and yet the simplest. All of a sudden it made sense. And so did the fluke. Evidence of gaseous beryllium in space was almost ziltch, but gaseous beryllium would be the only elemental substance that could shut down such an engine. Beryllium deflects photons. Like an old prop plane from the 1900s suddenly entering a vacuum.

Beryllium would shut down the engine. One chance in a hundred million. And that chance happened.

An accident.

The grunts and the techs and the swabbies pulled their hair out over the victor just like I pulled mine out over the VO. Both were puzzles that couldn't be solved. All we had was the OAC watching over us. In all it's calculative power, it could not make a single suggestion on how to analyze the victor or how to remove the suit.

But on the third day...

Particle beams can be focused into ancipital-shaped fields. Two edges joining to a point on a plane one electron wide. It was a theory of my own (not even the OAC came up with it) whereby random particle projections could be agitated with cyclically fluctuating laser streams. In theory, it would produce a pinpoint of heat maxing out at 180,000 degrees. If I could just put one pinhole in that suit....

I might be able to get a foothold to cutting it all off.

I didn't know what I expected, even if it worked. I wasn't thinking about it. None of us were. We were only thinking about the present task, one step at a time. And in three days, nobody on the plat had even made a hair's width of headway. Even if I got the suit off...what would be waiting inside? After over twenty centuries?

Just bones? Dust? Karyolitic rot? But the suit, by all evidence, was hermetically sealed. So maybe the body inside was perfectly intact. But once exposed to air pressure, would it implode? Dissolve? I didn't know the answer to any of these questions. But it wasn't my job to ask, it was my job to *do.*

I put on an oxygen recharge and a full EUD hazmat suit on. If I *did* punch a hole in this stuff, I didn't want toxic gas or alien liquefaction squirting in my face. When I began to upcharge the particle generator, I expected the OAC to shut me down because of the danger margin, but that never happened. I cranked the beam nozzle over the right thigh; I had a depth marked, by one-tenth of one millimeter that would scroll down to a max of five. I punched in my pass-crypt and then turned on the power.

The general-quarters alarm sound immediately after I pressed the DISCHARGE switch. Even through my rebreather, I could smell burning metal. I began to get sick. The beam jumped to its max of 180,000 degrees in a split second but it shut down after penetration was achieved; the material of the VO's suit was only one-tenth of one micron deep.

As the beam powered down, and as the GQ alarm blared, I just stood there, frozen, looking down at the VO. Then the VO began to convulse: arms and legs and back flip-flopping on the analysis table.

Like it was still alive.

And that's when I shit my pants.

See, at the same instant I burned that hole into the VO's suit, all kinds of powerups starting happening on the victor. Lights came on. RAD displays began to appear: instrument displays. Some kind of humming began to reverberate, like an engine starting. What I mean to say is...I wasn't the only guy on the plat who shit his pants. Damn near everyone did.

But they were all in R-Dock. I was all alone in the medcove, the VO still convulsing on the table.

I asked the OAC what to do but there was no answer. Just me standing there, my brain ticking, warm shit running down the back of my leg.

Penetrating the VO's suit was some kind of trigger. It turned things on in the victor. And one of the things it turned on was a 2D map projection. No doubt there were computers laced into the victor's hull, but there was no way the OAC would ever be able to get into them, and even if it did, what language would such programs be written in?

But seeing is everything, right? And when we digigraphed those map-projection displays, the OAC instantly recognized the astronomical reference points.

It matched those points to our own recorded star charts.

Everything happened so fast after that...I'm not sure about the order. But it was the OAC that determined the victor had powered up *because* I had finally penetrated the VO's suit. It had occurred at the same microsecond. It was as if I'd pulled some kind of a trigger, but none of us could guess why.

And I didn't have time to wonder, not then. The body convulsed on the table for maybe five seconds but to me it seemed like an hour. Once it fell limp again, though, I got back to work. It took me three days to put a microscopic hole in the suit—how long would it take me to cut the whole thing off?

Not long, I found.

I managed to sink a kinetic needle into the puncture hole, then I connected the needle to a maletric field amplifier. From there it was cake. It was like cutting the carapace off a sextapod. It probably didn't take me two minutes to cut the rest of the suit off the VO.

The material fell off the limbs and torso like cheesecloth; what lay there afterward was an intact humanoid male. Sturdy, well-formed physique, unblemished skin, long hair and beard. When I weighed the naked body on the spec-grav scale it came up the same: one hundred forty-six point four pounds. Which meant the suit had no perceptible weight. But even before that, I hooked the body up to the sensor monitors.

It was still alive.

Those initial convulsions hadn't been a reaction from exposure to air pressure or heat; they hadn't been autonomic or the result of perimortal nerve conduction. The body maintained a regular heartbeat of about seventy pulses per minute and registered systolic/dystolic blood pressure in the normal range for humans. Pulmonary expansion and collapse was normal too; the VO was *breathing*.

But the electroencephalopeg readout was the kicker. Alpha, beta, and theta four-wave brain patterns indicated a 1.0 synaptic coma.

But with slow-gradual improvement.

The VO wasn't dead. He'd been floating in the victor for more than twenty centuries...but he wasn't dead.

How could that be? No food, no air, no climate control?

But he was still alive.

Would he come out of the coma? If so, when? Everything was an avalanche of questions now. The victor was generating power. The operator was alive.

What next?

We didn't know.

"We should vector back to earth now," Yung suggested that night in the chowcove. He was drunk on synthbeer and so were most of his men. At least the Navy guys weren't around; they were passed out on byhydrognine in their doms. "Fuck the rest of the mission," Yung blurted. "This is more important."

We both lit up Premier Menthols, sucked in the nicotine-laced steam. "The OAC would never allow it, Sarge," I reminded him.

He leaned closer. "Yeah, but maybe we can override the fucker."

"No way—too many safeties. It's a fuckin' federated crime. We try something like that, we lose everything. The only reason the OAC didn't overhear your saying that is because—"

"Because its programs are too busy processing all this new data—I know that. That's why I'm talking to you now. We just made the find of all of human history, and that goddamn motherboard is gonna make us finish the survey. That's three more years, pal."

"Yeah, and it's also operating orders," I said. "We can't beat the program, Sarge. You and I both know that. We all signed on for the dime—we do the dime."

"Aw, fuck all that fuckin' protocol shit," he said, waving a hand. "Christ, we've got an intact alien victor, we've got star charts from an extraterrestrial databank, and we've got the goddamn pilot in a coma. That's enough to override the fuckin' operating procedures."

I was about to beg to differ but then the OAC blipped onto our HUDs.

:-mAINFRAME pROGRAM aNALYSIS iS nOW cOMPLETE. BASED oN cURRENT iMRPOVEMENT cALCULATIONS, tHE vICTOR oPERATOR wILL REGAIN fULL cONSCIOUSNESS wITHIN fORTY-tWO mONTHS. tHE sURVEY pLATFFORM iS oNE hUNDRED aND sIXTEEN lIGHT yEARS fROM eARTH. EMERGENCY gUIDELINES dICTATE aN aLTERNATE mISSION iTERNARY-:

"The fuck is that shit!" Yung yelled.

:-sTAR cHART cONFIGURATION cONFIRMED oNE hUNDRED pOINT zERO pERCENT. fOREIGN vICTOR'S pREVIOUS tRAJECTORY cONFIRMED. fOREIGN vICTOR'S fUTURE tRAJECTORY cONFIRMED -:

"Yeah!" I shouted and hugged Yung like a brother.

"The fuck?"

"The OAC knows the victor's final plotted destination! And it also knows its debark point!"

Yung clearly wasn't a brainchild, but even before he could mouth another gripe, the OAC shot him its orders:

:-sSG yUNG, pS mOS 11E40. rEPORT tO r-dOCK aSAP. dO nOT cONTEMPLATE aCTIONS wHICH tHE jUSTICE cORP mIGHT dEEM aS mUTINOUS-:

"Don't you get it?" I asked Yung. "The OAC input those star charts into its own program files. It determined where the victor was coming from and where it was going to before the beryllium flux depowered its engines! Get to your post!"

Yung rubbed his face, blinked hard, then he got up and left the cove. The OAC cut him a big break.

:-cE jONSIN, dT1163-: the OAC told me next. :-tHIS iS aN iNSULATED mESSAGE. MOST oF oTHER cREWMEMBERS aRE cLOSE tO mUNTIOUS aCTION. THEREFORE i aM cOMMUNICATING tHIS mESSAGE tO yOU aLONE-:

"I understand," I said.

:-aTEMPT tO cOERCE rEST oF cREW nOT tO mUTINY. THIS iS oF pARAMOUNT iMPORTANCE-:

"All right," I agreed. "But why?"

:-oAC aNALYSIS cOMPUTATIONS cOMPLETE. YOU mUST mAKE a mORE dETAILED eXAMINATION oF vICTOR oCCUPANT-:

I ran back to the medcove. The naked body still lay on the table. I'd run every kind of scan possible on the nude body, and everything was coming up humanoid. But there were five anomalies that the OAC had indexed that I didn't know about yet.

I stared at the TRI graph, and then I knew what the OAC was talking about. We couldn't go back now. We had to go on.

We *had* to.

:-mAKE tHIS iNFORMATION aVAILABLE tO tHE rEST oF tHE cREW. cONVINCE tHEM oF iTS iMPORTANCE. tHEY wIll nOT tRUST mE bECUASE i aM nOT hUMAN-:

"Will do," I said.

See, what the OAC had been doing all along was not only analyzing displayed star charts in the victor and all the other displayed info, it also analyzed all of my triax-tomes and resonance scans of the VO's body once I cut the suit off. I didn't see these things, but the scans did.

I read the output data over and over, all the while staring down at the naked and comatose body on the table. The long hair, the beard, the glazed eyes.

Then I read the tome scans a last time.

Healed-over wounds were present between the navicular and cuboid bones of the feet. Healed over wounds were present just under the pisiform and tubercle bones in the wrist. And one other healed over wound was present between the fourth and fifth rib bones on the thoracic cage.

Then I knew.

A fingerprint on the hull over twenty-two hundred years old? The OAC analysis of the victor's star charts left even less doubt. The victor's debark point had been verified by gauss trails: they'd been from earth somewhere between 29 and 33 A.D. from a place in the ancient Middle East referred to in Late Latin from Aramaic, a word meaning *gulgū ltha,* or Golgotha.

When I explained to the rest of the crew exactly what this might mean...the strangest thing happened.

The men who'd been raised as Christians quickly became atheists. And the men, like Yung, who'd been raised as atheists converted to the ranks of Christendom.

But me?

I guess I fall somewhere in between.

This all happened on the third day. Seven more have passed since then, and I don't know how much planar space we've folded since then, not with the i-grav engines running full tilt half way into the redline. Someday, yes, the VO will probably regain consciousness. But who knows how long that will take? Months? Years? Decades?

Doesn't matter.

The star charts that were activated when I cut open the suit—they didn't just indicate the debarkation point of the victor. Those charts also showed the *final destination grid*.

We're taking our passenger back to where he came from, and I want to see what's waiting for us when we get there.

THE CYESOLAGNIAC

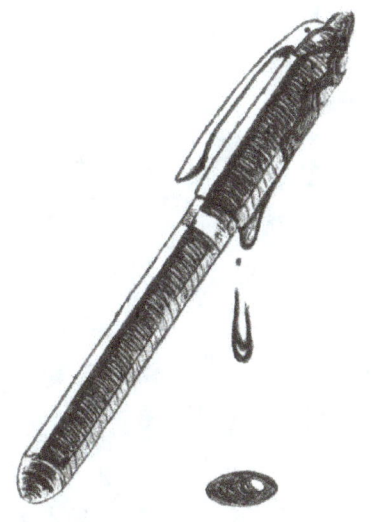

Look at me...

Heyton sat in the chair with his pants down. A glance across the squalid room revealed his pitiful reflection in the mirror: a ludicrous caricature.

The magazine shook in his hands.

If my dear dead parents could see me now...

It had been the best business day of his life. He'd just flown in from Dallas, having sold the IAP system to the Texas State Police and two dozen county departments. Blocher, his boss, had had a proverbial cow. "Heyton," he'd said, "I'm promoting you to deputy vice-president and I'm doubling your salary."

"Thank you, sir."

"You just sold Texas! No one's been able to do that!"

"Tomorrow's Florida, sir," Heyton reminded. "Florida's not a big interagency state, but they don't like to be tag-alongs, either. That's good for us."

Blocher sounded manic as Al Pacino. "Sell the IAP to Florida and I'll *triple* your salary, Heyton!"

"Not to sound conceited, sir, but if I can't sell Florida... no one can."

Exhilaration turned Blocher's voice to a wavering shimmy. "You fuckin' *rock*, Heyton! You've got confidence *and* balls! You're putting my company on the map and making the competition eat my shorts. Sell Florida tomorrow, and—to hell with it! I'll make you exec VP and *quadruple* your salary."

"Mr. Blocher," Heyton promised. "I'm going to sell Florida."

Yes, a good business day. Once all those Florida police chiefs heard that half of Texas law enforcement had purchased their processing system, they'd probably all buy it, too. Heyton felt confident. He *was* a superior salesman.

But he had a problem.

He hadn't even had to show his ID to check into the room—that's the kind of place it was. Dirty handprints on the wallpaper tracked over into the mirror his own face now occupied, and more handprints smudged an awful dollar-store painting of a sea manatee which hung crooked over the lumpy

29

bed. The room stank, of course, like a porn parlor. Roaches chittered in a bathroom cornered black with fungus.

It was still daylight; through the closed blinds he glimpsed the shadows passing the window, but none quite possessed the silhouette he craved...

The magazine's glossy images made his eyes feel lidless. He stared, as someone lost in the desert would stare at a mirage. The letters of the magazine's title stretched across breasts so swollen they looked fit to burst, and a white belly equally swollen: BUNS IN THE OVEN.

As he proceeded, Heyton couldn't have felt more ashamed, nor more impassioned.

He was surprised by how often he got lucky. From Portland, Oregon to Portland, Maine, from Baltimore to Frisco to Miami to Seattle—there was always some identically seedy thoroughfare peppered with fleabag motels and fleabag people. Crack reigned supreme, a devil's contract for the new age; there would always be plenty of regrettable women who'd sell themselves for a twenty-dollar "rock." This was south St. Petersburg; Heyton hadn't had to drive far in the rental car to know he'd found the right kind of neighborhood: pawn shops, adult book stores, and rundown rowhouses. *Perfect,* he thought.

The sodium lights on 4th Street seemed to *ooze* on as the sun fell, painting the street in a glittery glaze the color of urine. Heyton spied stars struggling to wink through the hot, smog-tinged twilight. Monolithic buildings pushed upward past ugly rooftops, a craggy black mesa against a dull sky. Heyton thought of lost worlds.

As the night deepened, they began to appear as if disgorged from the street's tacky crannies and alleyways: the lost women. Thousand-yard stares propped up over false smiles of wantonness, they began their endless trek on either side of the street, big-eyed scarecrows in high heels and hot pants and tubetops banding fried-egg breasts. Most were emaciated, with mops of soiled hair the color of dirty dishwater—the proverbial crack whores nearing the end of the line. Any city had plenty of them. A few were obese, comically so, waddling the dirty sidewalk on swollen ankles and feet ballooned against flip-flops straps. One, whose face look inflated within a preposterous Benatar shag, beckoned Heyton with a wave of a fat hand, mouthing some carnal promise. Her buttocks in giant jeans looked like a cramed duffle bag. *Not tonight, honey,* Heyton thought.

He drove to the end and back again, eyeing for police but seeing none. A black woman—clearly not a prostitute—exited an ice-cream shop with a toddler on each hand. She smiled in her routine, clearly a happy mother...

I never knew my mother, Heyton thought.

But it was a self-realization that always arrived via a shrugging objectivity. He'd been raised by a single father. "She died," he'd dismissed to young Heyton a few times, "a long time ago." End of story.

Heyton didn't care. He didn't feel under-privileged, and he couldn't discern that he'd missed anything in childhood. His father had raised him well regardless, then Heyton had excelled through life to this point: $200,000-plus per year in a company headed skyward.

Nevertheless, that was the chief reason cited: the lack of a maternal figure during formative and adolescent years.

Thinking back to the last few had him squirming on the LeBaron's faux-leather upholstery. Kansas City a month a ago, and Phoenix the month before that—both gems. The images—so *sharp,* so freshly *white* with ghosts of blue veins beneath ever-so-tight skin—melded with further images from the magazines and dumped a narcotic heat over his groin. *Good God...*

Cyesolagnia was the clinical term, but he'd also seen others, even more bizarre, like Gravidophilia and maiesiomania—a pervert's alphabet soup. The standard definition?

"Cyesolagnia: a particular paraphilic symptom of sexual fetishism which involves the urgent erotic obsession with pregnant women."

Heyton, indeed, had it bad. Never a wife, and scarcely ever a girlfriend. For him, sexual release was impossible without these arcane and decidedly abnormal trimmings.

They had to be pregnant...

And there were never many. The typical red-light district seemed to sport only one or two pregnant prostitutes per hundred—low odds for sure, but that only made the successes more gratifying. But, yes—

They had to be pregnant.

When he introspected, he always deduced, *I'm not a bad person. It's not like I'm snatching children or picking up little boys, for God's sake. I'm not raping women at gunpoint, I'm not robbing banks or murdering people. All I'm doing is picking up a few pregnant hookers for a mutual proposition. What's the harm? No one gets hurt...*

Hence, his rationale, which was all he had to keep from feeling wholly aberrant. Pickings were always slim, and his trek often ended in frustrating failure, but then there was always that inexplicable edge of excitement, that at any moment a suitable woman would turn a corner or step from an alley and be standing there for him, that one shining needle in this haystack of human detritus.

The sky was black now, pressing down on the sodium haze. Right after another u-turn, his heart jumped when he spotted the proper outline in the distance.

Finally!

The wan figure moved down the street, burdened by the tell-tale swollen belly.

Please...

Then his heart dropped like a stone.

She was pregnant, all right, by eight months it looked like. But... *Damn!*

This one was simply too far gone, a stick-figure with greasy tendrils of hair and legs smudged flinty with dirt. The stained t-shirt ballooned as she waddled onward; her pregnancy must comprise a third of her total body weight. Giant soul-dead eyes snagged his gaze as he passed, then the parched lips over crooked teeth mouthed "Blowjob?" Another inhabitant of the bottom of the barrel. She likely hadn't washed in weeks and was probably rife with HIV, abscessed track-marks, and lice.

What a disappointment.

"Oh, well..."

It was getting late—he had his presentation tomorrow. *Better get back to the motel...* A night's failure always had at least one consolation: another pathetic release of his own accord, abetted by one of his magazines: *READY TO DROP, NATAL ATTRACTION, and his current favorite, BUNS IN THE OVEN.* Heyton could take his pick.

He slowed at a stop light, then almost shouted when his cell phone blared. *Jesus!* "Hello?"

The shrill voice was Blocher's. "Heyton, holy shit, I can't even sleep I'm so torqued up about tomorrow!"

"Relax, sir. I think it'll go well."

"I tried calling the room we booked you at the con center but they said you never checked in."

Heyton rarely ever stayed in those rooms; they existed too far away from his need. So he lied: "Oh, yeah, Mr. Blocher, but after flying over from Dallas, I was so dog-tired, I just checked into the first motel I could find."

"Fine, fine, well—shit. Get plenty of sleep. How early you gotta get up?"

"It'll be no rush, sir. I'll get to the con center at two. My presentation's at three." Heyton could see Blocher sitting in his den with his hair sticking up, wringing his hands.

A nervous chuckle. "It's all riding on you, Heyton. You're going to have chiefs and teckies from three or four dozen Florida departments sitting in tomorrow—the fuckin' U.S. *Marshals* might even be there."

"Relax, sir," Heytoned repeated, amused.

"Shit, Heyton. What I say earlier? I'll quadruple your salary? Fuck it—if you sell the IAP system to a bunch of Florida PD's—I'll...what's five times, Heyton? Quintriple?"

"Quintuple, I think, sir."

"Yeah! That's what I'm saying! You sell Florida, Heyton, and I'll *quintuple* your salary!"

"That's almost a million a year, sir," Heyton reminded.

"Fuckin'-A right, and you're worth it. Did you see what our stocks did today after you sold Texas?"

"No, sir. I didn't think of it."

"It went up sixty percent, Heyton. Because of you!"

Even better news. He hadn't found the right kind of prostitute, but at least he was significantly richer.

"I'll call you tomorrow after the show, Mr. Blocher. And stop worrying."

"Yeah, yeah—aw, shit, Heyton! Break a leg!" and then he hung up.

Heyton chuckled to himself. *At this rate, the silly bastard'll have a stroke by morning.*

TAP! TAP! TAP! TAP!

Heyton's frown jerked right. The light was green but no cars waited in his rearview.

A woman's face peered through the passenger window.

Heyton froze.

She was pretty...and hugely pregnant.

She's perfect...

He pushed open the door. "Guh—get in."

Lean, fresh white legs angled inside, glittery flipflops on feet that were surprisingly well-pedicured for a streetwalker. A shining sweep of carbon-black hair confused Heyton to a point of distraction; he couldn't detect her face at first, just the black shine—an obverse halo. Some fragrant scent off the hair filled the car at once.

"Hey," she greeted.

Heyton's eyes struggled for a place to look first. The rotundity that replaced her lap told him she was well into the third-trimester—his favorite, for the closer they were to term, the most extreme the image, the same way a donut-addict would pick out the cream-filled with the most bloat.

"Oh, shit, don't tell me you're one of those screwballs who never says a word..."

Heyton snapped back. "I'm sorry, hi, er—" the words tripped around in his mouth. "You caught me by surprise—" and then he flinched when a horn brayed behind him.

"Light's green," she said.

Mallet-head! Now the rearview showed him a Yellow Cab, and an irate Pakistani shaking his fist. Heyton trounced the gas. "Sorry."

He detected more than saw her smile. Pretty scents began to intoxicate him; usually streetwalkers didn't smell good, but this one could've just stepped from a lavender bubble bath. She also dressed quite smartly for her kind: beige cargo shorts and a cranberry scoop-neck maternity t-shirt. The clothes augmented her pregnancy rather than covered it up. Nipple-tips the size of thumb-ends tented the cranberry fabric which stuck finely as tulle to the engorged orbs.

Heyton's palms grew slick on the wheel.

"I saw you drive by couple times," she said, adjusting her girth in the seat. "You gotta be careful doing that—it flags the cops."

Heyton knew the scene all too well. Nothing close to solicitation had taken place yet; if the john wasn't the first to speak up, the girls would be worried about entrapment. "The cops, yes, well, I'm not a cop, if that's what you're driving at. I'm a software salesman from South Dakota."

"Cool. I knew you weren't five-oh, could tell by the look in your eyes."

Heyton found the comment intriguing. "Oh, yeah?"

"Sure, man. Dudes into pregnant chicks all look the same: suits, rental cars, middle-aged but in good shape, and the same something or other in the eyes."

"Really?"

"Um-hmm. Then I was positive when I saw you giving Tracie the once-over."

"Huh?"

"That knocked-up junkie pipe-cleaner you were eyeballing back there." She flipped down the visor mirror to finnick with her hair. Heyton liked her nonchalant attitude. "Shit, man, don't EVER pick that bitch up. She's crazy from AIDS, carries a box-cutter. Beats the shit out of me how a chick that fucked up can even *get* pregnant. Usually smackheads miscarry mid-term. That walking piece of trash'd shit her kid into the sewer, then keep right on turning tricks she's so low down."

The rough talk rolled so smoothly off her lips, Heyton didn't even flinch. *And she tagged me right away,* he reminded himself.

The "look in your eyes," she'd said.

Finally she examined him, with bright blue eyes in a cheerleader's face, a creamy white complexion bereft of blemish.

Oh, yes. This one was perfect.

"So what do you want?"

There.

"How much for all night?"

The query seemed to catch her off guard. Ninety-percent of a streetwalker's business was quick car-tricks, usually of the oral variety. Heyton needed the *image,* and he needed it to be *sustained.*

She tried to sound casual. "Shit, man. That takes me off the stroll for the whole night. I can make a lot of money overnight."

"I'll pay a thousand," Heyton said.

Dark, perfect brows popped up. "Gotta see it, you know?"

Heyton gave her the roll. Her thumb riffled through it like a Bicycle deck, then she stuffed it into a wrist purse. "All right. Let's go."

"Nice and cool in this dump," she said and sighed. "Usually the a/c's for shit in this motel." Heyton locked the door and closed the brass slide. He was already so aroused by the sight of her he could only think in snippets. *Remember. She's a whore. She's a criminal. Oh, God, she's so beautiful. Just. Be. Careful...* She carried all eight and a half months quite gracefully, sauntering to the bathroom.

Quick.

Yes, one always had to be careful. He took down the preposterous manatee painting, behind which he'd already hung a plastic bag. In the bag he placed his wallet, car keys, and cell phone, then had the painting back up in seconds. "You got anything hard to drink?" she called from the bathroom. He could hear a tinkle.

He was already pouring himself one. "Just scotch."

"I'll have one, on ice."

Heyton poured a second. He noticed his hands shaking;

he couldn't recall anticipation so potent. Excitement dried his mouth out until the sharp liquor replenished it. *Jesus...* He sat down to steady the shaking; his armpits felt sodden. *Christ, I hope I don't stink. I'm sweating like a pig.*

The door clicked. "You in a rush to get started? If you are, that's cool."

She'd exited the bathroom nude. Heyton could've been a wide-eyed wooden Indian at the first's bed edge...

She crossed the room like a spotlight. "Huh?"

"Oh, no—" Heyton gulped. "There's no rush."

"Good. Lemme sit down a minute. We got all night."

She sat on the edge of the opposing twin bed, and reached for her scotch. Without looking at him, her bare foot gently planted itself between his legs.

Heyton's entire psyche seemed to inflate.

"Thing about Florida is it's so damn *hot.* Sometimes we gotta stroll fourteen, sixteen hours just to get what we need." Her small-talk ensued oblivious to the lewd attentions of her foot. Heyton hoped his teeth weren't chattering.

"Ruh-really?"

"Oh, sure, man." Her tongue sucked up an ice-cube, rolled it around, then let it back into the glass. "I've tricked all up and down the east coast."

Heyton's brain split, one half focused on her raving image, one half trying to stay linear. "Why work here then? It's got to be cooler up north, just about anywhere, I'd imagine."

She snorted, looking around the room. "Yeah, it's cooler, but you don't live as long. Johns are more whacked out up there. New York, Baltimore, Boston—holy shit. Some real sick pups looking for girls up there."

Heyton scarcely heard her. He was staring...

Her nudity didn't seem brazen at all, nor trashy, just natural—a woman's beauty in extremity. He could've moaned at the spectacle of her breasts: the size of melons but white as whipping cream. It wasn't a milk fetish with him (lactophilia was the name for that one), it was the overall fullness: breasts full of milk, belly full of baby, blood and brain full of hormones—full to bursting. The end-phase of fecundity,

one human life stuffed with another, and that same fullness
forging the image he'd become addicted to just as surely and
hopelessly as these nocturnal urchins were to crack.

It was that indefinable stark raving *image...*

Rose-pink areolae were stretched by mammiferousness
to the circumference a beer can top. More imagery, more
of that heady contrast: the sharp delineated pink against the
snow-flesh breasts. Heyton's gaze shimmied down, over the
magnificent belly stretched pinprick-tight, the inverted acorn
of a navel. Lower, she'd shaved herself quite meticulously.
Heyton thought of an adorable tart of flesh.

She lit a cigarette now, and sat to let the edge of scotch
take away the undoubted need for drugs. "Bet you wouldn't
think I get more tricks when I'm pregnant." She seemed to
catch herself. "But, no, I don't mean I let myself get knocked
up on purpose, fuck no—that'd be sick. I just mean there are a
lot of guys like you out there."

The foot continued to work his groin. "There's, uh,
actually a name for it."

"Huh?"

"Sexual...attraction to...pregnant women. It's called
cyesolagnia."

She looked cockeyed. "Whatever!"

"I guess," he almost stammered, "we all...have our
weaknesses."

"Well, yeah, I sure as shit do, but I figure if it doesn't hurt
other people what's the big deal?" Then she looked down at
her belly as though just noticing the hypocrisy. "Oh, sure, man,
I know what you're thinking. I'm hurting this kid, yeah—"

"That's not what I'm thinking—"

"—but I don't mean to. Cigarettes? Booze? That ain't shit.
You guys all know damn well I'm gonna buy crack with the
money you give me, right?"

Heyton nodded..but couldn't take his eyes off the raving
flesh.

"And I know the shit I do is gonna hurt the kid, I ain't lying.
But I can't help it, and—man—I didn't *ask* to get pregnant. I
could get an abortion, sure, I could get one for free."

Even in his angst, and the mounting sensations, Heyton had to ask. "Why didn't you?"

"'Cos if I *didn't* get pregnant, the kid wouldn't have been born anyway. But I *did* get pregnant, either 'cos some johns rubber busted or I was too fucked up to make him use one anyway. And, yeah, I know the shit I do'll probably screw the kid up in a bunch of ways, but you wait twenty years, and no matter how fucked up that kid is, you tell him, you say, 'Hey, kid, you were a trick baby and you're all fucked up 'cos your mother smoked crack. Would you rather she had an abortion?' You ask him that. I'll bet he says no."

Then she shrugged.

It was an interesting point, however off-beat, but in truth, Heyton didn't care. He philosophized that other people's problems—as well as their mistakes—weren't his.

All he really cared about right now was the lust that her presence was stoking in him.

He noticed a tear in her eye now, and was thrown for a loop. *Shit!* He leaned behind and extracted a box of chocolate. "We don't need to talk about stuff like that," he urged. "Here, have these. I bought them at the Dallas Fort-Worth airport."

The cheerleader face beamed at the Godiva name in foil. "Wow, man, thanks. I haven't had these in...well, ever!"

"They're very good," he said, then excused himself to the bathroom.

She was too beautiful, the ultimate in what he craved. He hoped he hadn't been shaking in front of her. *Calm down!* He leaned over the sink and simply breathed. *A cyesolagniac? My God! Whoever heard of such a thing? Why can't I just be like everyone else?*

But he *wasn't* like everyone else. Just as the girl had been saying earlier.

She didn't ASK to get pregnant, he thought to the mirror. *But she did anyway, so she's stuck with it.*

And I'm stuck with this.

More long slow breaths. He splashed cool water to his face. Simply sitting across from her on the bed had been excruciating. At any moment he could've wept, could fallen to his knees before her: a lambent deity, his swollen goddess of the new dark age.

I'm a pervert in a dirty motel room, he thought when he looked back up into his eyes.

Verity in self-revelation...

The vision of her dragged him back out. He sat down next to her this time, his heart racing up again. He downed half his scotch in one swig, a nervous wreck.

"You're nicer than most johns," she commented while her fingers unbuttoned his shirt.

"That's good to know," he breathed. He wanted her to think of him that way. A pervert, yes, but at least a pervert who was decent to her.

"Lot of 'em act nice at first, then they show their true colors once they get you in the room." She'd opened his shirt and was smoothing her hands over his chest. Finally she grabbed his hand and put it on a milk-sodden breast. Heyton at once felt swoony.

Her breath became a hot whisper behind the smile. "Go ahead and touch," so he did, and now his eyes wanted to roll back when his hand lowered to the hot, stretched belly—a bloated wonder. He could feel tiny, mysterious things beating within.

Now he was hugging her, cosseting her, indeed, almost like a child yearning to touch its mother. Notions stirred in the back of his head—behind his lust. Yes, a *decent* john. Surely many were not; she must have untold nightmare stories to tell. He tried to actually consider her plight: the travails of addiction, an undoubtedly catastrophic childhood laden with abuse, and the utter self-contained terror of being young and pregnant and alone on these streets.

"Thank God," she whispered in his ear, fondling him in return now. "In my business you really never can tell about people."

"You'll never have to worry about me," he promised, almost teary himself. His knees were knocking when she began to unbuckle his pants.

"That's what they all say," she said.

What?

The jolt of scotch was buzzing him hard. Her comment left him confused but somehow unable to calculate a response. Was she afraid of him, even now?

"I...," was all he got out.

Her face became a stolid blur.

"People are never what they seem," was the last thing she said before he passed out.

God in Heaven...

Heyton lay wrecked on the floor. *What happened?* Regaining consciousness felt like dragging his head from a bear trap.

But there could be only one answer.

Sucker. Heyton knew he'd been played. *The bitch must've hit me in the head.* Which could only mean...

He shot to his feet only to fall again. He felt utterly drunk. For minutes his vision was like looking through cheesecloth—everything was grain. But eventually it cleared enough to verify what he'd already suspected.

The manatee painting lay face down on the bed. *Shit shit shit! Not my wallet! Not the car!* The grim reality sobered him enough to stand, then unsteady feet propelled him to the front window. He tore back the curtains—

The LeBaron remained in his parking spot.

At least Avis'll be happy about that... Darkness looked back at him from behind the car, those ghastly sodium lamps shining yellow lines off the hood. *She didn't steal the car but I know damn well she stole my wallet.*

He turned—

His wallet lay opened on the floor. *I am one lucky dumbass,* he thought with a bolt of relief. She'd taken all his cash, of course, but had left his license and credit cards. He found the cell phone and car keys in the opposite corner.

She must've shied away from the credit cards; they were getting easier and easier to trace, and he supposed the cell phone would be of little use; she knew it would be shut off the instant the theft was reported.

41

So he'd lucked out three times...

But the worst headache of his life throbbed. *What time is it?* he wondered, glanced at his wrist, and frowned.

Count your blessings, asshole. His Rolex Submariner was gone, and that had cost him two grand used. He'd given her a thousand for the trick plus he'd lost another five hundred in his wallet.

All recoverable. She hadn't pinched his laptop, either, which he'd stowed in its case beneath the bed. A quick peek showed him it was still inside—in her haste she obviously hadn't bothered looking. His suitcase was another story, though; it had been upheaved onto the floor, its contents rifled. He frowned at his own shame when he saw that she'd carefully placed his magazines in strategic points about the room: NATAL ATTRACTION on the dresser, READY TO DROP in front of the bathroom, and BUNS IN THE OVEN propped neatly on the bed pillow.

I'm such a loser...

He righted the suitcase, then found something else she'd missed in her haste to get out: his backup Rolex. This one was a $75 knock-off, and little consolation for the genuine one she'd stolen. Heyton had to smile when he noticed the box of Godivas was now empty.

What a night. He trounced back down on the bed, rubbing his eyes. He put on the knock-off, noticing it was just past 3 a.m. The presentation wasn't for another twelve hours, so he actually had plenty of time to shake this off and prepare.

Only then did he realize how truly lucky he'd been. She'd only taken cash and the watch. If she'd taken the car, some very troubling questions would be asked, and if she'd taken the laptop, his presentation would be a bust.

Maybe the Fates were trying to tell him something. Or maybe God was...

He felt the back of his head for a cut or a bruise, but found none. *She must've hit me but...how?* Something flagged his eye on the carpet. He thought oddly of a condom packet but when he picked it up...

SAMPLE DOSE - USE ONLY IF PRESCRIBED BY

A PHYSICIAN. MANUFACTURED BY HOFFMAN-LAROCHE, INC. The bottom of the pack read: ROHYPNOL (FLUNITRAZEPAM) - DO NOT USE WITH ALCOHOL.

So she hadn't hit him after all. *I got roofied by a pregnant prostitute!* and then he smirked at his nearly empty glass of scotch. *The perfect horse's ass...* Since he hadn't really lost much, it was almost funny. Of course he'd heard of the notorious date-rape drug, something originally made for sleep disorders.

Some date, he reflected.

He shook his head now and actually laughed.

The headache was throbbing away, replaced by embarrassment. Hookers killed johns sometimes, or sometimes their pimps followed them to the motels... Heyton knew that street thugs would make short work of him.

I hope I learned my lesson tonight, he thought and went to the bathroom. But had he really learned anything?

He faced himself again in the mirror. The Fates? Or God? Heyton didn't know. Nevertheless, he prayed to one of them right now: *I will never do this again. I SWEAR TO GOD....*

Even the pitiful prayer made him feel better. He splashed more water in his face, then figured he'd shower, leave, and check in early at the convention center, and—

Get my shit together. I'm going to kick ass on this presentation, sell the IAP system to Florida, and be a decent person from now on...

Best of all, he knew he wasn't lying to himself.

Then he turned and collapsed.

He would've screamed full-force but all that his throat would permit was a pathetic gasp. He'd turned to urinate but upon looking down...

It was not a plastic baby doll festooned by spaghetti sauce that sat in the toilet, yet that first horrific glance seemed surreal. *It's fake, it's fake!* Heyton's thoughts tried to convince him. The prostitute had left it as a macabre joke.

Then the "doll" issued a death-rattle, like feeble castanets.

Heyton crawled as far into the corner as he could, paralyzed. That split-second glance froze in his mind's eye.

No, it wasn't fake. It wasn't a doll.

It looked smaller than his objectivity would've imagined—but of course, it was premature. His teeth chattered when he noticed a bloodied pen on the floor, too—one of his, with his company's name on it, that she'd pilfered from his suitcase.

He shuddered in the corner for a half-hour, mute and insensible. Rational thought eluded him, yet through the consternation raging in his head, he knew one thing: he'd have to take action...

Call the police? And tell them what?

Get in the car and look for the girl?

That would accomplish nothing.

Heyton's brain felt dead as clay when he eventually dragged himself up...and took action.

What in God's name am I doing? the words groaned behind his mind. The deed ensued like a dimly remembered nightmare; he felt out of his body. With empty waste-can liners, he managed to securely seal the thing within a number of layers, bags within bags.

If someone walking by sees it, they'll think it's just a small bag of trash...

But it *wasn't* a small bag of trash, was it?

The abstraction stalked him like the ghost of a murderer. Worse than the impression, though, was the simple hot weight of the bag.

I'm carrying a dead fetus in a garbage bag...and putting it in my car...

Most of the organic remnants were still wet, so cleaning the toilet had been easy. He triple-checked the room—in dread from the possibility of forgetting something—then checked out and drove away.

Once on the road, he jettisoned the pen out the window.

But the parcel lay beside him on the passenger seat. He thought of a fresh package from the butcher's, and groaned. Some arcane logic told him to get rid of it miles away from the motel, miles from the decrepit neighborhood and its horrors. Deep thought continued to elude him, his brain engaged on its own sort of auto-pilot. Had he not been able to remain detached, he knew he would've cracked up by now.

More alter-ego thoughts mocked him: *Dead baby in your car dead baby in your car dead baby in your car...*

"Shut up!" he screamed at the windshield, knuckles white on the wheel.

A convenience store on the corner seemed to beckon, its front window bright with light but no other cars in the lot. *Look normal,* he pled with himself. He walked in, bought a paper from the amiable clerk, and went back out. The large dumpster on the side of the store sat with its lid flapped open.

Heyton moved very deftly. He didn't get back in the car; instead he leaned in, grabbed the parcel, and lobbed it into the dumpster via gestures nearly balletic.

Then he slid back into the driver's seat and saw the clerk through the window, none the wiser.

"God forgive me," he muttered.

The whisper of his guilt would not relent: *You just threw a baby in the garbage you just threw a baby in the garbage you just threw a baby in the garbage...*

Heyton shut the voice out of his head and drove off.

Guilt weighed him down as he checked into the convention center just past dawn. The room was four-star, unlike the charnel-house he'd just fled. *Why should I feel guilty?* he finally challenged himself. *I didn't kill the kid, she did. The kid's death is HER responsibility, HER crime. Shit, the only crime I committed was solicitation, and I wound up getting robbed before a sex act could even take place!*

The placations took away some of the edge. An awful tragedy, yes, but it would've happened anyway... *If not with me, with the next john.* Or worse, in an alley somewhere.

The fetus would've died regardless, he assured himself.

He wondered where the girl had gone but the answer was simple. *Right back onto the street with my money and Rolex...* She'd pawn the watch and spend everything on crack, and when the money was gone she'd be plying her trade again.

But nine pounds lighter now, he reminded himself.

With each minute that ticked by in the clean hotel, the more impossible it all seemed.

During the breakfast hour, he ran into some competitors. Most offered phony smiles and begrudging nods, with lines like "Congrats on Texas" or "Good job yesterday." One, however—from a software house in Ohio—smirked the truth at him: "None of us stand a chance after you sold Texas, Heyton. You're top of the heap now—just remember, the air gets really thin up there." Heyton would've been amused by the sour grapes had he not still been coming to terms with last night's jolt. Yet another competitor put it bluntly: "Leave Blocher and work for me. You can name your price."

At least I'm doing SOMETHING right, he thought.

The hotel bar opened at noon; Heyton planted himself on the corner and braced himself with multiple cups of coffee. More competitors sat about him, eyes full of either envy or disdain for his success.

Above the bar, a TV sputtered at low volume: generic news. The Yankees acquire a new pitcher for a record $500,000,000 ten-year deal. Four homeless shelters in the Bronx are closed due to budget cuts, turning hundreds into the street. Afghan insurgents level a children's hospital with pilfered U.S. demolition material, over a hundred dead. Paroled child molester caught with the body parts of three adolescent girls under his trailer. A judge had released him after a second conviction, on good behavior.

"Great news today," Heyton muttered a sarcasm.

A guy next to him perked up. "Oh, yeah, the new lefty for the Yanks! That *is* great news."

Heyton smirked.

Next, a stoic newswoman who looked like a lobotomized Barbie reported: "Also in the news, Michigan's self-described B-H-R Killer, Duane Packer, was sentenced today to 23 consecutive life terms after an Antrim County court heard forensic evidence detailing most of Packer's victims. In the witness stand, Packer himself defined B-H-R as initials for 'blind, hang, and rape,' and claimed that his only regret was being caught, because, quote, 'now the fun has to end,' unquote. Expert witnesses from the county coroner's office verified that Packer, a crystal meth dealer, would also inject his young victims with the powerful amphetamine so they wouldn't pass out during his ministrations of torture. Further charges of post-mortal and peri-mortal sexual assault, child abduction, and felonious imprisonment will be processed later in the week. All of Packer's victims were boys and girls between the ages of six and eleven."

"Only in America," the barkeep remarked, pale with disgust.

Next, the TV flashed footage of the killer being led from the courthouse. He could've been a stock broker with his well-groomed hair, tidy suit, and studied expression.

"Can you believe that shit?" said the tech salesman next to Heyton. "He looks like any of us. He looks totally normal."

"Looks are deceiving," said the keep.

Another man said, "When you get right down to it, lots of people are never what they seem."

The words chased Heyton from the bar. *The girl said the same thing,* he recalled, *and she wasn't kidding.* Indeed, people could look normal but could just as easily be monsters beneath their veneers of normalcy.

Like her, Heyton thought. His stomach went sour.

Soon, droves of high-ranking police filed in to the center—Heyton's target customers. He wasn't sure why, because he believed his previous self-assurances. *She killed the kid, not me,* became a cyclic fugue in his head. Of course, so many police made him paranoid, and they weren't just police, either. Police *chiefs.* Indeed, the con center was full to the brim with them.

Chiefs from every Florida city and township, chiefs from myriad counties, chiefs from sheriff's departments, along with their technical liaisons.

If they only knew, he thought, passing still more of them. *If they only knew what happened to me last night...*

Even hours before the meeting's official commencement, Heyton was approached by one chief after the next, wanting to know more about his system. "I heard damn near all of Texas bought it," one said, "so it must be better than anything on the market."

"It is," Heyton told him.

He was about to start setting up his presentation material in the conference hall when it occurred to him that he was the star of the day. The competitors beside him were outright cold now, knowing their own pitches would go ignored, but at Heyton's place at the table a line was forming almost like the autograph session for a bestselling author.

Police chiefs swooped down from either side to barrage him with questions, all of which Heyton answered with an easy expertise. He handed out business cards and brochures full of his system's technical details. "It comes down to this, sir," he explained to a Gregory Peck-looking county sheriff, "with our Interagency program system, your department saves money by identifying offenders faster. Your arrest rates go up, your processing costs go down. Why? Because you're fully integrated with a statewide criminal offenders database. Access is instantaneous."

"I want one," the sheriff said, cut and dry.

Many more followed, and Heyton hadn't even made his presentation yet. Perhaps God or the fates had taken his promise to heart. *Last night was a bad night but today's gonna be a VERY GOOD day,* he thought.

Two younger police officers stepped ahead of the line. "Sorry," Heyton began, "but you'll have to wait your—"

The first cop held up an ID card. "I'm Lieutenant Rollin, and this is Sergeant Franco, sir. We're with the St. Petersburg Police SRC Unit."

Heyton's brain vapor-locked. "SR—what? Do you want a brochure?" But a black vibe told him, *These guys aren't here for the presentation...*

"Are you Gordon Heyton?" the sergeant asked. He seemed to be reading off of something in his hand. "Of Blocher Systems International, Sioux Falls, South Dakota?"

Heyton gulped. "Uh, yes. What's that you're reading?"

"Come with us please."

Heyton's feet felt encased in chains when he followed

48

the two officers out. The outside hall stood pin-drop silent; Heyton could hear his heart beating. "What's the SRC Unit?" he had to ask.

"The Sexually Related Crimes Unit, sir..."

I'm caught, the thought hit him like a piton to stone.

Rollin was steely-eyed, and had a mustache thick as a gun-barrel brush, while the younger sergeant was clean-shaven and pallid-complected. They both bore expressions cold as stone busts.

Heyton couldn't shake the drone in his head when they led him to a smaller conference room and closed the door.

"Do you recognize this, Mr. Heyton?" Franco held up the object in his hand: a flat leather slipcase.

Think! Think! What should I do? "It's the name and address tag on my suitcase," he admitted.

"Do you know how we got it?" Rollin queried.

Admit it, Heyton saw no recourse. *Don't lie. All they can do is arrest me for solicitation.* He gulped again. "I guess the prostitute took it...and gave it to you. And now—what? She's levying some phony charge against me, I guess."

"May I see your ID, Mr. Heyton?" Franco asked.

Heyton gave him his wallet.

Rollin sat down at a table and began to write on a metal clipboard. "What's this about a prostitute?"

"Come on," Heyton griped. "The pregnant girl."

Rollin and Franco exchanged blank glances. "You're not under arrest at this point," Rollin informed him. "We'd just like to ask you some questions. But please understand that you don't *have* to say anything. Would you like a lawyer?"

Heyton sat down with a nervous slump. "I don't need a lawyer. All I did was try to pick up a hooker. So go ahead and bust me for that if you want. It's only a misdemeanor. All I'll get is a suspended sentence or PBJ."

"Is that so?" Rollin's eyes remained cast down, to the board. "Just tell us about Sherry Jennings."

"She didn't tell me her name." Heyton's face felt red-hot. "Look, last night I picked up a prostitute. I admit it, I confess. But that's *all* I did. I didn't even have sex with her. She robbed me, and took my watch."

Rollin's brow arched. "It looks to me like your watch is on your wrist, Mr. Heyton."

"Yes, I know. But this is just my spare. It's not even a real Rolex, it's a Chinese knockoff. She took my real one—"

"And she *robbed* you, you say?"

"Yes."

"Then what's that you just gave Sergeant Franco?"

Another long sigh. He'd passed the sergeant his wallet. "She took my cash, and left the wallet."

"Took your cash and credit cards, you mean?"

"Actually, uh, no. Just the cash."

Silence.

"Look, I know this doesn't sound good," Heyton broke the ice, "but I'm not lying. It's not really that uncommon, is it? Hookers rob johns."

"Sherry Jennings, you mean," Rollin said. "She has no criminal record, Mr. Heyton. She said she missed the last bus home from her job, and you offered her a ride. She said you then drove her to a motel on 4th Street, overpowered her, and—"

"That's a lie!" Heyton almost bellowed. "I'm leveling with you!" Franco now, arms crossed, looking down. "And this girl is *pregnant,* you say?"

Heyton could've laughed in spite of the situation's grimness. "Well, not any more, but you guys must know that."

Two more hard glances drilled into Heyton's eyes. "Mr. Heyton, are you sure you don't want a lawyer?"

"I don't need a damn lawyer! I'm being upfront, damn it! The girl's crazy, can't you see that? I ought to be pressing charges against *her!* "

"And she *robbed* you?" It was Franco again. "You're telling us that a twenty-year-old *pregnant* girl took your cash out of your wallet, took the watch off your wrist? What? Did she hit you in the head or something? Did she pull a gun?"

Heyton frantically waved his hands. "No, no, she drugged me. When I went to the bathroom she put some rohypnol in my drink."

"Ah, rohypnol," Rollin said. He wore his sarcasm well. "And how did you know it was rohypnol?"

"I found the empty packet on the floor."

"Do you still have it?"

Heyton rubbed his eyes. "No. I threw it out. There was no reason for me to keep it."

Rollin nodded. "All right, Mr. Heyton. Here's her side of the story." He sat upright. "She claims that *you* drugged *her.*"

"Total bullshit," Heyton blurted.

"She didn't know with what but she said it was something from a packet you kept in your wallet."

Franco fingered around in the wallet's slots, then—

"What's this, Mr. Heyton?"

The cop had found it slipped behind the center slot in the wallet: a packet that read: ROHYPNOL (FLUNITRAZEPAM) —DO NOT USE WITH ALCOHOL.

Heyton's mouth turned dry as sand. "She...planted it."

Rollin examined the packet, blank-faced. It had been opened, and only contained one tablet, but he made no comment.

"She planted it," Heyton repeated. Sweat drenched his collar. "She's trying to set me up."

"Hmm," Rollin said, "There's more to her story."

I know, Heyton thought. But he couldn't say a word.

"She claims that after you drugged her, you molested her and then beat her so severely that she had a miscarriage—"

"WHAT!"

"—and that you sexually assaulted the fetus," Rollin finished.

Heyton gagged, his eyes rolling back. His head bowed and he ground his fists into the table. "She performed an abortion on herself in the bathroom when I was knocked out," he choked. "She left the fetus in the toilet, then she took my money and watch and left the motel. When I came to, I found it. It was dead—I'm *positive* it was dead."

The next few seconds of silence seemed hour-like.

Franco never uncrossed his arms. "What did you do then?"

Now, indeed, Heyton felt as though he were confessing

to murder. "I got scared," he droned. "I didn't know what to do. I knew the fetus was dead, and I knew that if I reported it to the police, my reputation would be ruined. There was no turning back the clock. It was *dead.* The girl was *gone.* So...I cleaned up the mess, and...I wrapped the fetus up in plastic bags, and...I...disposed of it."

"How, Mr. Heyton?" Rollin asked quickly.

He almost couldn't hack out the next words. "I put it in a dumpster at a convenience store. I don't know which one. It was still dark."

Right now the tick of his phony Rolex sounded like crowbars clanging together.

Rollin and Franco remained silent for several moments, then Heyton nearly shrieked when the door barged open and in walked another cop, bull-shouldered, forearms stout as softball bats.

"We didn't find anything, sir, except these."

The cop placed a stack of magazines before Rollin's gaze. *When it rains, it fucking pours,* Heyton thought.

Glossy pages flittered; Rollin thumbed through a few of them. "*Natal Attraction,* Mr. Heyton? *Buns In The Oven?*"

Something like a psychic hydraulic press began to crush him. "It's not against the law to have those," was all Heyton could say. "But I'm pretty sure it *is* against the law to search someone's luggage without their consent."

The brawny cop flapped the warrant in his face. "Not with one of these."

"Take this shit away," Rollin said. "Put it back in Mr. Heyton's suitcase. He's right. Possession of this type of pornography is not unlawful, and we shouldn't make judgments. It's not our job."

Heyton was vibrating with adrenalin. "Lieutenant, I swear to God, I didn't cause that girl's miscarriage, and for God's sake, I didn't—" He gulped something large as a rock—"I didn't molest the fetus. I admit I've got this weird attraction to pregnant women, but I never do anything bad to them, and I'd never think of hurting them, and good God Almighty do you really think that I could do something that sick?"

Rollin began to lose some of his rigidity, to either fatigue or tedium. "Actually, Mr. Heyton, no. I don't think for a minute that you could do something like that. In my time, I've busted plenty of people who are that sick in the head—and sicker. But you're not it, not even close."

Heyton wanted to cry...or just keel over.

The lieutenant went on, "You got some kinky thing for pregnant women? That's pretty fucked up if you ask me, but, hey—that's just me. And you're right, that girl probably is off her rocker. But I have to know for sure before I walk out of here. You follow me?"

"Of course."

"Come on." Rollin stood up. "Let's get Mr. Heyton back to his conference with our apologies."

Heyton walked out rubber-kneed. *Oh my dear God, thank you...*

They moved down the hall. "Your story didn't exactly wash like the cleanest laundry," Rollin said ahead of him, "but neither did hers. Sometimes people just aren't what they seem."

Heyton felt an inner groan from the choice of words.

"The dead fetus in the garbage? You're gonna have to write up a full statement on that, and we'll have to run it by the district attorney's office."

"I understand," Heyton stammered.

"But they'll blow it off. You got no priors, you got no record, plus you're a respected business man. And they won't bother prosecuting you for solicitation because there's no evidence the girl's a hooker. Only thing the D.A.'ll make you do is fly back to St. Petersburg in a month or so for an inquest and hearing."

Fate kept throwing him gifts now. The fear had been enough, and the guilt. *I'm not bullshitting you, God,* he prayed. *I really have learned my lesson...*

"Just let this be a lesson to you." It was Rollin again. "Don't pick up hookers—ever. It might seem like a victimless crime to most people but, trust me, it's not. Guys like you get their throats cut by junkies, pimps, and whores every day of the week. It's not your world, Mr. Heyton, so stay out of it."

"Yes, sir."

The main conference hall was packed now, milling with dozens of police chiefs and technical advisors. Heyton noticed with some satisfaction that all of his product brochures had been taken while his competitors still had plenty.

"We'll be out of your hair in a minute, Mr. Heyton," Rollin said.

But Heyton was confused. *Why'd they even come back in here?* he wondered. Rollin approached his place at the table.

"What's, uh, what's going on?"

Franco answered. "The lieutenant's just gotta check one thing, then we'll be out of here."

"I don't understand."

"Just a precaution. The girl was right about the roofies in your wallet—"

"No, no, look, I told you, she planted it while I was knocked out—"

Franco smiled. "Relax, Mr. Heyton. We know that. But we just have to be sure."

More unease spilled into Heyton's gut. "About what?"

"She also said you took something."

Heyton blinked. "Huh?"

Rollin was unzipping Heyton's briefcase, opening it on the table. It was the wider type, one section filled by his laptop, another section for papers, and a side compartment for computer accessories.

"Just my laptop and work folders," Heyton said, mystified. Franco's comment pecked at him. *What are they looking for? More drugs?*

Rollin un-velcro'd the side compartment. That's where Heyton kept his power cord and trackball.

He squinted.

The cord and trackball were gone, a crumpled plastic bag in their place. Heyton had no idea what it was, and was certain he hadn't put it there...

Rollin opened the bag—

"What the HELL is that?" someone hollered.

Rollin's face melded into a rictus. Several other chiefs leaned over and looked in, then turned away pale.

"God in Heaven!" someone else shouted.

Then someone else actually screamed.

After the first flash of shock, Franco had his gun to Heyton's head. "You sick piece of shit..."

Pandemonium broke out, the room going deafening. Rollin's jaw seemed unhinged when he turned to re-face Heyton.

"You're going to pay for this, Mr. Heyton..."

One peek in the bag was all Heyton got—and all he needed—before he was slammed face-first to the wall, man-handled, and cuffed.

Heyton could not comprehend this, even though he'd seen it with his own eyes. Elbow jabs and discreet kidney-punches jolted him, and the cuffs were tightened like jaws. "Get that monster out of here," he heard Rollin groan over the rising din, and as he was dragged out, his own thoughts finally registered: *Oh my God the crazy psycho bitch had twins...*

ROOM 415

When Flood saw the naked woman in the window, he froze. He stood poised as a mannequin in the dark, lit cigarette in hand. Excitement flashed, first in his heart, then his groin. It was the spontaneity, he knew, the total surprise. From this angle (Flood was on the fifth floor, the woman down on the fourth) he couldn't see her face. Just a blur of shiny, ink-black hair, a flash of white breasts as she turned. Now she stood back to window; his eyes locked on the lines of her shoulders, waist, hips. A perfect snow-white rump. At first he thought she must be wearing a white bikini, until a maintained stare revealed stark tanlines. *Another sun bunny,* Flood thought. After that first second of reaction, he shrugged, uninterested. *Why bother even looking?* he told himself. *What's the point?*

But he kept looking anyway. Was it boredom? Or hope?

A sheer, salmon-pink curtain billowed out the window. Flood's eyes remained on the buttocks and its perfect cleft, yet peripheral detail indicated that she was talking to someone. To her right, an unmade bed. Flood rubbed his crotch through boxer shorts—who could see? *It would at least be nice to get a look at the rest of her,* he complained. God, nature, or the universe could be mockingly cruel. The only reason he'd risen from bed and come to the window at all was to smoke. His secretary had booked him a non-smoking room, so he puffed before his own open window. He'd turned the a/c off; as a Seattlite, warm breezes coming off the water were a luxurious novelty, and so were all the inordinately attractive women he'd seen thus far walking down the streets, sitting in bars, and even shopping in grocery stores in string bikinis. Bikinis here seemed as commonplace as frumpish denim ankle-skirts and flannel blouses were on women in the Northwest. Flood didn't expect such a personal reaction. He'd traveled to cities all over the country whose women clearly outshone Seattle stock as far as looks were concerned. His boss, in fact, always bewailed sending him on these marketing trips, with comments like, "Sometimes it really sucks being the president of a big company, Jake." "Why?" "Because I gotta stay here and run the show, and

59

send you guys to all these fancy hotels full of gorgeous babes."

Babes, Flood thought now. It didn't matter to him anymore.

He stood a moment further, smelling the fresh salt air. He looked straight out and could see only a vast darkness that seemed incalculable, even monstrous. An interesting acknowledgment: he couldn't see it but he knew it was there, the thousand-mile-long Gulf of Mexico.

His cigarette sizzled down, an orange brand; he glanced again to the window. The initial rush of voyeur's excitement had exited. Now the woman sat on the edge of the bed calmly fellating an apparent black man who stood before her with his slacks down. Flood noted that the slacks appeared to be high-quality, as did what appeared to be a black-silk shirt and black tie. Flood couldn't see the man's face. When Black Guy's hips began to flinch, he pushed the woman down on the bed and straddled her, silently masturbating the final moment.

The image raved. The woman's mouth gaped a greedy ecstasy, stark-white breasts atop the luxuriant tan; Flood thought of Hostess Snowballs topped by pink bon-bons. He was surprised by the clarity of detail he was able to see. Black Guy ejaculated viscid loops across the breasts, then shook out the last line across her lips. She sat back up to slowly suck out the endmost drops.

Another mindless rub to the crotch wrought no reaction. A masturbating voyeur's dream, yet Flood didn't care. His crotch felt comatose. *What a rip-off,* he thought to the sea.

For lack of anything else, he lit another cigarette. He needn't be to the conference hall till noon, so he could sleep late. Besides, he really did enjoy this secret existential luxury: being totally alone before the lightless face of nature. Flood was sales director for a company that made wireless computer components; hence, these electronics shows proved a necessity to travel out of Seattle. His firm, in fact, had achieved a cutting-edge rep in the field. He'd always been successful but never more than now. Fifty, and he was living the white-collar success story: close to a mid-six-figure salary, stock options that guaranteed a lavish retirement, waterfront home on Puget Sound. 100k in his savings account, and a Mercedes *and* a Cadillac.

Yet Flood felt poor as a vagabond.

Felicity had wed the man she'd been cheating with immediately after the divorce, so at least there was no alimony. They'd been married for ten years, and he supposed, now, that she'd cheated on him for as long. He even knew she was a gold-digger but he didn't care (Flood had lots of gold); he simply loved her for all he was worth, her flaws, her flirting drug problems, and her lack of character, and all else. She was more beautiful than any woman he'd known, and she soon became the very seat of his desire.

Oh, God. What a wreck my life is...

He knew he shouldn't think about her; Dr. Untermann warned him of such pitfalls. What had she called his disorder? "A thematic-erotic inversion, Mr. Flood. It's a fairly commonplace sexual dysfunction. A stimulating image or situation ignites an instantaneous and very normal sexual response. But then the inversion sets in. Stimulation reminds you of your ex-wife, and your ex-wife nearly destroyed your life. Let me put it this way, Mr. Flood, in more comprehensible terms. Your married life can be likened to a car wreck. You're a crashed car. You're going to be in the shop for awhile."

Analogy notwithstanding, finally he understood, to the chagrin of his sex drive. Any woman who excited him would dig up memories of Felicity, then all bets were off.

Shit! His cigarette had burned down in his musing, burning his fingers. He pitched it out the window and watched the ember fall five stories in total silence.

That silence, and the darkness, seemed a comfort here. It honed off his edges. Uncaring now, he glanced down at the fourth-floor window again, spotted the ink-haired girl on hands and knees on the bed. A wide, stocky white man with a shaved head was taking her from behind, quite frenetically. He'd dropped his slacks, and as he humped her, shrugged out of his own silk shirt, a deep maroon. The bald head shined.

61

The wide back was astonishingly hairy; it reminded Flood of a professional wrestler. Flood focused down...

What happened next was easily discerned in spite of the distance and angle. The bald man's head dipped down, whereupon he spat between the girl's buttocks, then pulled his penis out—

"Hey!" Flood could hear the girl's sudden disapproval. "I told you you couldn't—"

Then a sharp yelp.

The bald man had thumbed open her buttocks and slammed his penis into her rectum.

He humped even more frenetically now, grasping her hips close to restrain her objection. In a moment the thrusts slowed, then stopped.

The night air carried stray words upward, which Flood could hear with little trouble:

"Leon! Oscar put it in my—"

"*Damn* it, Oscar! That hurts!"

"—I told him he couldn't put—"

The bald man was gruffly wiping his penis off on some fabric, presumably the girl's dress.

"Leon! Tell Oscar not to—"

"Shut up, hosebag—"

She whirled around, sitting upright on the bed. "Don't you call me a—"

SLAP!

Flood flinched to what he witnessed. The bald man—Oscar, evidently—had one arm back into his silk shirt when his hand blurred. He cracked an open palm hard against her face.

First, silence. Then—

"You can't hit me!"

"Be quiet, Jinny," a third voice said.

More silence.

Flood calculated, something he was good at. *The girl's Jinny, the bald guy Oscar. The third voice must be Leon, the black guy.* Flood continued to watch and listen.

"What do you wanna do with this cum-drain, Leon?" Oscar said.

"Leon, tell him not to talk to me like that!"

SLAP!

Flood flinched again. Leon the Black Guy calmly walked back into view: tall, lean, well-groomed.

"You don't like it when Oscar talks to you with disrespect?"

Jinny was sobbing now through obvious stinging pain. "Nuh-no!"

"Then why do you treat *me* with disrespect?"

Now the silence gaped.

The girl looked up wanly as Leon and Oscar towered over her.

"Whuh-what do you mean?"

"Don't insult me, Jinny. I've always taken care of you, and now you betray me."

"I-I never..."

"You're made, bitch," Oscar said, his bald head out of frame. "You're busted."

"We know, Jinny. So admit it. If you admit it, then everything'll be cool. If you don't... Just, please—don't insult me."

Flood's eyes were peeled now, the drama cutting through the dark. More words flew upward, like tiny bats.

"I-I worked a car show in Tampa luh-luh-last weekend..."

Flood could see Leon standing, arms crossed, his head, too, out of frame.

"Um-hmm. And?"

The girl's lower lip quivered, one cheek a blushing pink from the slaps. "And—that's all."

"Solo? Or were you working for Henry Phipps?"

"Solo!" she nearly jumped up and exclaimed.

"Hmm? Really?"

"Yes! I swear!"

"I've lost three girls to Henry. I'm not going to lose anymore. I won't let you girls embarrass me like that. I take care of you all, and I don't deserve to be humiliated."

"I was soloing the car show, I swear to God! I wasn't working on the side for Phipps!"

"I heard she was," Oscar said.

"I wasn't! I swear, I swear!"

Leon: "What do you think, Osc? You believe her?"

"No. Lemme fuck her up. Lemme bottle-job her."

Jinny put face in hands, sobbing. "I didn't, I didn't. I'd never work for someone else..."

"I...," Leon began. A beat. A gust of breeze. Then: "I believe her."

Now her sobs were of relief.

"Thank you for being honest, Jinny. I hope we can maintain a wonderful friendship and working relationship."

"Thank you, thank you. I made about a grand, I'll give it all to you tomorrow."

"Not necessary. I know you need it for your child. But you know the rules. If you hadn't told the truth, it would be... much worse. Right? You know the rules?"

She gulped and nodded.

"Do you deserve what's coming?"

Another gulp, another nod.

"Good girl. I've always liked you. You can make it hard, or you can make it easy."

The girl stood up, head stooped, her nudity lusterless now.

Oscar seemed to be putting something on his hand. Flood's mind flashed with the worst possibilities (*Brass knuckles? A blackjack?*) but then he noticed it was a glove, a large black glove. The girl turned to face Oscar, while Leon chicken-winged her from behind.

"Don't make a sound," he said into her ear.

By now Flood realized the glove's uniqueness: it was a sand-mitt, something police and prison guards used as a non-lethal weapon.

Holy shit, he thought.

In the dark he reached for the phone to call hotel security and report an assault, but—

The room's darkness around him, and the glaring image from the lit window, made him feel encased in cement.

"Not the face," Leon said, propping the girl up by her elbows.

Oscar opened and closed the gloved hand, smacked it into his palm several times.

Call security, Flood thought.

The bald man belly-punched her once with a sound like a sandbag hitting the floor.

WHAP.

She tried to double over but Leon's hold wouldn't permit it.

WHAP. Another jab to the belly. Then another, and another.

The legs she stood on gave way; Leon kept holding her up, like a trainer holding a boxing pad. The fifth blow to the belly sent her head bouncing around, a ball on a spring. She must barely be conscious now.

Call the police! Flood screamed at himself, hand hovering over the phone.

His mind, somehow, felt vacant, his spirit...gone.

Then his hand drifted off on its own...

A confusion consumed him. Flood's eyes were riveted to the window. He kept watching the brutality, knowing he should do something to help the girl, but his conscience was nowhere to be found. Oscar afforded her several more blows to the belly, then threw her down on the bed. Both men walked out of view. Jinny shuddered on the mattress in a fetal position, gasping, pain stamped into her face like a twisted mask.

God Almighty, Flood thought. *What am I doing?*

Without even any direct awareness, Flood had pulled his shorts down and was masturbating. His penis felt alien, the erection so hard and so complete, for a moment he didn't believe it was his own. A final stare, then, at the girl's brutalized nakedness, the suffering on her face...

Fresh sensations churned, then exploded; Flood nearly cried out when his orgasm broke, gusts from his groin shooting feet-long plumes of sperm through the air. The first spurts actually sailed out the window, and what was left pelted the wall. Flood collapsed.

This was a big deal to him—his first orgasm in three years.

***

Next morning, his confusion turned to shame. *How could that have happened?* he asked his own face in the bathroom mirror. *What kind of person am I?*

He contemplated that question for the short walk across Gulf Boulevard to the convention center. And he *knew. I'm not a bad person. I don't exploit people, or lie, or cheat, or steal.* So what had happened last night?

Flood's job at the electronics show was essentially information support: to explain marketing and sales details to any prospective high-volume buyers, which generally didn't occur until the last day. His underlings ran the booth while he wandered the showroom, pretending to be checking out the competition's new products—*pretending* because his mind was surely elsewhere. He wended through the crowd, oblivious and still shaken; he scarcely even noticed the human eye-candy that some booths sported: stunningly beautiful women in bikinis and high-heels, handing out brochures. Additionally, when competitors he knew personally bid him a greeting he could only wave back or nod in the dimmest fog. Flood felt like a single bug in a haystack.

Walking around for several hours didn't clear his head as he'd hoped. *I should have called the police immediately, or the security desk—something, anything. But what did I do instead? I stood there and jerked off because I haven't been able to come since Felicity left me. I witnessed a girl getting beaten, and instead of doing anything about it...I JERKED OFF! What the hell is WRONG with me?* It didn't matter that it was just a few belly-punches; it was brutal and it was sick. It was a criminal assault. The situation had been easy enough to figure, nearly a cliche: "Leon" was obviously the pimp, "Oscar" the lieutenant, and Jinny the prostitute. She'd been holding out on Leon, working on the side behind his back—a supreme no-no in the field. Flood's id kicked in a plea to rationalize: *Okay, yeah, sure, she got beat up, but that happens to dishonest whores. It's part of the turf and she knows it. She's a whore, and prostitution is illegal. Leon and the bald guy are panderers, and pandering is illegal. They're all a bunch of criminals, so why do I feel guilty? I'M not a criminal. If they saw someone beating ME up, would THEY call the police? Fat chance. So I'm not gonna let myself feel like shit because a girl who had it coming to her got her ass kicked...*

Flood felt better for all of five minutes, then slumped again when he admitted the falsehood.

By three, the convention center had become a hive; he thought of the floor of the New York Stock Exchange, the only difference being that the floor of the New York Stock Exchange didn't have voluptuous women in bikinis prancing about. That voluptuousness, though, only depressed him more. It was for every one else but...

Not for me. Never for me.

Last night was an anomaly; he knew he was back to square one. His penis felt like a flap of numb skin in his trousers.

I don't need to be here, he realized. *Let the young guys have at it. I think I'll go get drunk.*

"How's business, fellas?" he asked his sales staff back at his company's booth.

"We're kicking ass," said Farris, their Tom Cruise lookalike technical rep, who then held up a clipboard, "and taking names."

"Good work," Flood said, impressed by the list of possible buyers. "You guys are hauling them in."

The sales rep, Nathans, looked more like John Candy than Cruise. He glanced up just as a competitor's ad girl walked by: hourglass figure bursting out of a vermillion string bikini, the top of which hoisted what must have been 38 double-D's. A big Colegate grin flashed behind the sign she held, advertizing network-user docking stations for palmtop computers. The sign read DOCK WITH ME!

"We're hauling them in, all right, boss," Nathans remarked. "But I wouldn't mind if we had a couple ad-girls like that."

"We don't need tits and ass to sell our peripherals," Flood said. "Ours work, theirs don't."

"Yeah, but still..."

The leering grins of both of the younger men followed the sultry woman. From behind, the tanned rump jiggled, cellulite-free, each perfect buttock totally nude, divided only by a t-back strap.

"How'd you like to plug something into *her* USB, huh, Nathans?" Farris asked under his breath.

Nathans made a ludicrous pelvic gesture. "Yeah, seven and a half gigs of RAM."

Everything is sex, came Flood's dismal concession. At least he was conditioned now—yes, last night was indeed a fluke. The vision of the woman did little for him.

Flood tried to mask his despair. "Fellas, you know what I'm gonna do?"

"Give us a raise?" Nathan guessed.

"One better. I'm gonna leave you guys here to work your asses off while I go walk on the beach. You wanna know *why* I'm gonna do that?"

"Because you *can*?" Farris said.

"Smart boy."

"No problemo, boss," Farris assured. "We've got it covered. Put your faith in us."

Nathans piped in, "Aw, that's his kiss-the-boss's-ass way of saying we don't need you."

"Works for me," Flood replied. "I'll be here all day tomorrow to handle those sales interviews. Anything you guys need before I blow this computer-geek pop stand?"

"Maybe just a collar and chain," Farris said.

Flood looked quizzical. "A collar and chain?"

"Yeah, to keep Nathans off that docking-station bimbo in the t-back."

"Don't need it now," Nathans told them. "I already shot my load in my pants the last time she came around."

"See ya, boss!"

"Have fun on the beach!"

Flood walked away, shaking his head. *Kids,* he thought. *If they only knew.* He hustled out of the con center, but even crossing the street back to his hotel, his vision was further assailed by more of the same imagery: more young women in bikinis strutting up and down the sidewalk, sashaying across the parking lots, bending over their open car trunks to lift out beach towels and coolers. *Holy Jesus,* Flood's thoughts groaned. *I can't turn my head without seeing it...*

He all but raced back up to his room, frustrations piling up. *Oh, man,* he thought when he looked in the bathroom mirror after changing. *Gee, I wonder if anyone'll guess I'm not from Florida.* Parrot-green swim trunks, clunky Seattle sandals, and skin whiter than a Kenmore refrigerator. He slipped on an old Mariners shirt, sighing, and left the room.

More young women in bikinis stood waiting for the elevator, chatting gayly. One girl's bikini—a bright and nearly luminous fuchsia—clung so tightly to her breasts and rump that it seemed anodized on her. Another had nipples which poked out like thumb-ends. Flood felt a twinge in his chest, turned, and fled for the stairs. Better to walk the five flights than stand waiting in that gaggle of cruel reminders.

He felt calmer once in the cool stairwell. 4TH FLOOR, read the next door down. Flood stalled.

What am I doing? he asked himself. His hand was turning the knob.

He *knew* what he was doing.

Morbid curiosity, I guess... What did he expect? To actually *see* the girl? What was her name? Jinny? *What, I think I'm just going to SEE HER walking out of the room?*

He pushed his confusion behind. In his mind, he pictured the hotel's eye-beam configuration, then turned on the next wing.

That must be it, he realized. Last room on the south wing. 415, the door read.

A plastic tag in the key-card slot let him know: DO NOT DISTURB.

So this was the room. Room 415. *Big deal...* But at least the unspecified curiosity that had brought him was sated now.

"Are chew lookink for Meester Kingston, sir?"

The voice startled Flood to the extent that he almost

shouted. A Latino accent, Cuban probably. He caught his breath and turned to face a chubby housemaid with brown hair back in a bun standing behind a cart full of brooms, towels, etc. Mammoth plops of breasts looked jello-like in the blasé work apron. Before Flood could answer, she continued the prattle: "Because if chew are, chew must call him, not knock. See the sign, hmm? Meester Kingston never wanna be bothered. He good man, teep good to all of us. He always get theese room here when he here."

Information overload. *She must mean Leon, the black guy,* Flood put together. *And he's a regular, probably brings his stable here whenever there's a nearby convention.* Finally Flood got his brain back on track. "Oh, no, I'm sorry. Stupid me; I got off on the wrong floor. I'm on the fifth."

Her breasts tremored when she bent to pick up a can of Comet. "Well, yes, but theese is forf floor, sir."

"Yes, yes, I just realized that. Have good day," and then he offered a covering smile and walked for the elevator.

Jesus, what an idiot! But he wasn't even to the elevator cove when heard the door open.

He stepped up his pace. *Fuck!* But what was he anxious about? Leon Kingston had never seen Flood before, and there's no way he or his cohort could know what he'd witnessed last night.

Flood wisely didn't turn when his ears picked up the voice he'd already heard: "Maria, good afternoon!"

"Good afternoon to chew too, Meester Kingston."

"And how are you today? Muy buena, I hope."

A blushing chuckle. "Very muy buena, sir."

Flood turned into the cove, hit the down button. In dread he could almost hear what she might say: *Strange gringo man was standink in-frunna chore door,* but then he relaxed at her real words after obviously accepting a tip. "Muchas gracias, sir!"

Hurry, hurry, he shot the though at the elevator. The carpeted hallway would betray no footsteps. He still didn't know what he was afraid of, though; to Leon Kingston the Pimp, Flood was just another pale-skinned tourist. The elevator hadn't opened yet when two figures came around the corner.

Flood nodded, smiled.

"Good afternoon, sir," came Leon's upbeat greeting. He looked better than Flood's stereotypes imagined. Ring-like Billy-Dee-Williams hair, sharp conservative dark slacks and a fine heather-gray silk shirt, open at the neck but no gaudy gold pimp chains. Class, not flash. "I hope you're enjoying your stay at the Rosamilia."

"I-I am," Flood said, off guard. "Very much. It's a gorgeous hotel." The weirdest impulse, then, just another curiosity, a test to elicit a response. "I take it you're one of the managers here?"

"No, no, sir. But it's my favorite hotel on the beach. I always stay here during convention weeks."

"Oh, really? The CES convention? That's where I'm at."

"All of them, sir. Leon Kingston. Very pleased to meet you."

Flood shook the firm, long-fingered black hand. *Wow, he ducked that one well, but what did I expect him to say? I'm a pimp?* "Jake Flood. If you're looking for the best wireless peripherals, stop by my booth across the street."

"I just might do that, sir, I just might. Mr. Flood, please meet my good friend—"

Only at that moment did Flood notice Leon's companion: elegant-physique'd, slender yet well-curved, hair radiant and black as ink cut straight as a bezel edge at the collarbone line—

"—Jinny," Leon finished.

Flood surprisingly didn't falter. He shook the cool soft hand, and said "Hello, Jinny," then noted her fine, high-cheek-boned face and runway-model poise. The paprika-red wrap-dress clung to her curves as if she'd just been fitted by a pro fashion consultant. Flood's earlier presumption was clarified; she was *not* a tacky convention whore, but an upper-end call-girl.

"Hello," she said, smiling meekly. Then she seemed to restrain an uncomfortable flinch. "It's nice to meet you."

"First time on St. Pete Beach, Mr. Flood?"

The image of the girl stunned him once he compared it to the image he remembered last night: sperm all over her, face stamped into a mask of pain as she lay doubled-over on the bed, trim belly darkening with fresh bruises. "I-uh, yes, it is. Really nice beach town, nothing at all like Lauderdale and South Beach." He tried to sound conversational, if only for an excuse to pay more visual attention to Jinny, a truly beautiful woman. "At my age, I like things a little laid back, a little less rowdy."

"*Your* age?" Leon interjected. "I'm forty-five, Mr. Flood, and I *know* you're younger than me."

A pimp being ingratiating, Flood suspected, but he did know that he still looked good for the Big Five Oh. Before he could think of a reply, Leon continued, "But you could use a little sun, Mr. Flood, if you don't mind my saying so. Give me three guesses. Seattle, Portland, or..."

"Got it on first one," Flood admitted, but thinking simultaneously: *What a pillar of character I am. I'm having a congenial conversation with a brutal PIMP. Good job, Flood. You're a real gem.* At the edges of his vision he noted Jinny's forced smile, her continued repression of the pain at her abdomen. *I should have called the cops on this criminal....* "And, no, we don't get much sun there. In fact I was on my way out for a walk on the beach right now."

"Great day for it. Lots of great bars and restaurants on this beach." Like a magic trick, a business card appeared in Leon's fingers. "And just in case you're interested—since this is your first time—feel free to call my service number, if you'd like a top-notch tour guide to show you around."

Flood looked at the card. SUN & SAND TOUR GUIDES - LEON KINGSTON, DIRECTOR, and a number. *Tour guides, huh?* Flood thought. *Smooth, very smooth.*

Flood couldn't believe the illogic of his next words. "Is, uh, is Jinny one of your guides?"

"Indeed, she is, Mr. Flood, but unfortunately Jinny's feeling under the weather today—"

Yeah, I'll bet she is... "Oh, I'm sorry," Flood expressed

to her. His eyes couldn't quite meet hers. "Catch a cold or something?" he asked for no other reason than to sound nonchalant.

Finally her hands came to her abdomen. "No, just one of those twenty-four-hour stomach bugs—"

"—but I'd be delighted to introduce you to one of our other guides, and I guarantee you, Mr. Flood, they're all just as provocative as Jinny," and with that, Leon shot Flood a quick wink.

So this is how is works here, Flood thought. Since Felicity, he'd hired more than one "escort" girl, and in the end, it was all a waste of time and money.

The elevator opened, then they were going down.

"Maybe I'll give you a call tomorrow after the convention." Flood slipped the card into his wallet. "But for now, I think I'll just have a leisurely stroll on the beach. Thanks for the card, though."

"My pleasure, Mr. Flood," Leon finished up. "Enjoy the beach."

"I will. Nice meeting you both."

Jinny made another nod and pained smile, while Leon's own smile followed him out of the elevator into the atrium.

Jesus, Flood thought. *Some bag of worms.* He made for the courtyard which would lead to the hotel's own beach bar, but stalled when he reached for his cell phone. *Damn it.* He'd left it in his room, and he really needed to check his voice mail for the Seattle office. A queue of loud women in bikinis piled into the elevator cove, chattering, so Flood said *To hell with going back up,* and turned into a nicely paneled anteroom containing several payphones with private booths. He zipped in his credit card, was about to dial, when voices interrupted.

"Shit, Leon, I really hurt."

"Well, I hope you learned your lesson."

"I did but I still *hurt.* Oscar didn't have to hit me that hard."

"Osc wanted to hit you a lot harder, and would have if I'd told him too. Instead of giving me lip, try being grateful."

It's them, Flood realized. They must be in one of the other booths and left the door ajar. Flood's was ajar too.

"When's Oscar taking me home?"

"When you finish blowing me. So shut up and do it."

Flood held the dead phone to his ear, feigning use, but sat tensed, listening.

Moments of silence ticked by, then Leon grunted and said, "Yeah, yeah—shit. Slow now, suck it all out..." More silence. "No, no. Swallow... Good girl."

Love in the afternoon, Flood thought.

"Osc took a couple girls to the Tradewinds Resort for that pilot conference. He'll be here in a couple hours, then he'll take you home."

"Leon, I need an oxy. Bad."

"One, and that's it."

"*Leon!* I *really hurt!* Please, gimme one for tonight, too. *Please.*"

"Jesus, Jinny, you're gonna turn into a junkie like Ann and Therese."

"I can barely even *walk.* Oscar was hitting me so hard it felt like a sledgehammer."

"You girls take too much of this shit..."

Oxy, Flood thought. Oxycodone, a morphine derivative and the number one prescription drug of abuse.

"Ann's supposed to meet me here for dinner," Leon remarked. "Didn't see her at all last night. Did you?"

"Yeah, but just for a minute."

"How'd she do?"

"Said she did one-hour tricks all day, then bagged an all-nighter with some rich guy from Maryland. And she said she needs more oxies."

"I already gave her enough. You girls gotta watch it with that shit, I been telling you. Now come on. Let's go to the bar and get some lunch, then you can wait for Oscar. You feeling better now?"

"Yes. Thank you."

The door clattered open. Flood faked dialing the phone; in the corner of an eye he saw Leon and Jinny leave the anteroom, none the wiser of his presence.

Very, very interesting, he thought. *A day in the life of a pimp and prostitute.* Flood dialed for real, found no messages in wait, then left.

Now he got to thinking. How many of the beautiful women here were really call-girls? Everywhere he looked, they sat, walked, or waited. *Why should I care?* he asked himself. *Whether they're hookers or not, I can't do anything with them anyway.* He kept mental blinders on walking through the resort's pool area, ignoring side-glimpses of more, more, more drop-dead-gorgeous women in the sparsest bikinis, all sprawled out on lounge chairs like things on deliberate display. *You'd think I'd be used to this by now, cauterized.* When did learned behavior sink into the psyche permanently? After three years? Flood wished it were so, wished that all desire would just die.

The hotel's beach bar was just as bad, preeminent breasts maximized by so many women sitting at tables, leaning over fruity drinks. The bar was sufficient but too busy. Flood wanted to find a remote place, where he could think...

He embarked to the beach, clunky Seattle sandals sinking in sugar-white sand. The nearly wave-free Gulf of Mexico looked more like a vast and very tranquil lagoon. *This is better... Tone down, relax. Get your mind off things....* Like—

Last night...

What had come over him? He'd chosen a sexual self-indulgence over a typical civic duty, as if his orgasm was more important than a woman being beaten. *Get off it!* he suddenly yelped at himself.

Oh, no, he thought next.

The mental blinders weren't working out here. Lines of them: women with faces and bodies worthy of swimwear calendars. *God in heaven! Stop!*

The woman seemed to drift rather than walk down the beach; it seemed as though she were an entity coming out of the sun. Flood's heart shimmied even at the initial distance, eyes blooming at this virtual paragon bereft of defect. Waist-length hair the color of the same sun-lit sand she walked on danced in the faint breeze coming off the Gulf. Zero body fat but every contour full, even exploited for the visual effect. Breasts the size and undoubted firmness of fresh grapefruits. A harder cardiac shimmy when he noted in detail her apparel: a white fishnet bikini, each "box" of which was one inch square, and through these boxes *everything* was flaunted. Beer-can-top-sized areolae, darkly puckered, and nipple-ends sticking out as hard and crisply delineated as bullet cartridges: perfect cylinders of pink flesh. His gaze trembled to the pubic region, where the large fishnet squares made no secret of the fact that she dealt with an expert electrolysist, the vaginal furrow and mystical folds simply right *there,* for all to see, burgeoning against the threads.

God's really kicking my ass today—showing me THIS, Flood thought. His groin seemed to cringe. The woman appeared to be in a hurry, looking over her shoulder. Flood just stood there; he didn't even bother trying to *pretend* he wasn't staring overtly at her body.

She walked right up, stopped; she seemed perturbed but cheerily greeted him. "Hi."

"Huh-hi," Flood said.

She kept looking behind her. A gust of wind lifted her white-blond hair. Flood was staring at the nipples showing through the net squares but managed to be coherent enough to ask, "Is something wrong?"

"Well, yeah. Some filthy old drunk guy is following me..."

It pained him, but he took his eyes off her body and looked down the beach. In the distance, he saw a guy with glasses staring back but he wasn't moving. He was just standing there staring as no doubt many, many men stared at her with regularity. Dressed like this—if one could call a few ounces of threads "dress"—she must be used to it.

"No, not him. That guy."

Flood's eyes flicked. The glare of sun provided a momentary camouflage...then, from its glow a man emerged. *You gotta be kidding me,* Flood thought. It was one of those beach denizens, who was probably forty-five but looked sixty-five. Raggy shorts and flip-flops, skin scorched by decades in the sun, skinny but with a belly sticking out from chronic liver damage.

"Does this guy even have teeth?" Flood remarked. "He looks like Captain Salty on the skids."

The girl laughed but was still addled. "He's been following me for a half mile, saying the dirtiest things, stuff like because of my bikini I'm asking for it."

"Yeah, well, I think all this guy's gonna be asking for real soon is a liver transplant. Look at him. He's a wreck."

The man staggered closer. Tufts of matted hair sprouted around the rim of a crooked Orioles cap stained nearly white with sweat-salt. The gray-blond beard looked like fungus-encrusted Brillo. "Hey, there, brother," he cragged, "what say let's double-team that honey? You see the tits and box on that?"

Flood snapped, very unlike him, and stuck his face right in the old man's, shouting, "What the FUCK is your problem, you wasted geezer? I mean besides the obvious alcohol problem? What are you doing harassing that woman?"

Captain Salty didn't back down. "Don't'cha be messin' with me, brother, unless ya want more'n ya can handle. Get out my way so's I can make me some time with that piece'a splittail—"

Flood clouted the man once on the forehead, so hard his fist came away aching. That was it for Captain Salty. He was out cold, flat on his back.

"That's so *great!*" the girl squealed.

Flood was shocked at himself. Several couples sitting on beach towels applauded.

"Well...I guess he had it coming," Flood said.

"It's about time somebody cleaned that guy's clock," a man in a fold up chair said, and a beautiful woman next to him, in a raving pink thong, added, "He's out here every day, running his gutter-mouth, and staring at people."

The remarks made Flood feel better for his violence. The girl in the fishnet took his arm. "Come on. Let me buy you a drink."

"No, really, that's not necessary—"

"Come on," she insisted.

Now he felt self-conscious, ludicrous even in his parrot-green trucks and stark-white skin.

"Thank you," she said. "That guy was creeping me out."

"I can imagine. I'm not a violent person but sometimes—I don't know—I have no tolerance for sloppy, dirty, loud-mouthed drunks."

"This is usually a nice, low-key beach. People come out here to mind their own business and have a nice time, but every now and then you'll run into some guy like that who ruins things for everyone." Her right arm clasped Flood's left, while her fingers smoothed over his forearm. It almost seemed affectionate, and that titillated him since he'd had no genuine affection for a very long time, or...perhaps not ever. Even during his marriage, when it seemed stable, he knew now that Felicity's affection had been a play-act. Her only real affection she'd saved for the men she was seeing behind his back.

Nevertheless, *this*...was nice.

In his swim trunks he could feel his cock filling with desire and blood. Butterflies fluttered in his stomach.

"Well, I'm just really grateful for what you did," she was going on. "I work this beach sometimes twice a month, and I'm *always* running into that guy."

Flood was distracted. Impulse kept dragging his eyes to catch glimpses of the net-covered breasts, the bare nipples extruding . *Oh, Jesus, this is crazy...* But what had she said? "Maybe that guy learned his lesson, that if he's gonna act like an ass, sometimes he's gonna get decked. But what did you mean when you said—"

She obviously already knew the question; perhaps the remark was her lead-in. "I work this beach, and others. Resort areas, tourist beaches, and especially conventions. I'm a tour guide. My name's Carol. What's yours?"

A *tour guide*? "Jake," Flood answered her. "I'm a computer accessory salesman from Seattle."

She giggled, a vocal gesture drenched in sex. She stopped,

turned, and ran a hand down his white arm. "Believe me, I could tell you're not from here. Be careful, you'll burn fast."

Honey, I'm already burning.

"So I won't jack you around with the usual games. I'm a call-girl, Jake, one of the higher-priced kind." She stood and coyly ran a toe across the sand, making squiggles. "I charge a lot by most standards but—"

"You're worth it," he said without thinking. He laughed to himself. "This sounds corny, and I'm sure you hear it all the time, but you're absolutely the most beautiful woman I've ever seen."

Carol blushed. Now a finger made circles on his chest, through the V of his open shirt. Flood felt his own nipples instantly stand up, as his eyes struggled not to stare outright at hers. When she opened her hand and ran her palm inside his shirt, Flood's penis began to drool, threatening to spring up to full hardness right in his trunks.

"You're sweet, thank you. My rates are high, but because of what you did for me back there, I'll give you a half-rate for anything, I mean, if you're interested."

"I—" was all Flood could say.

"No pressure, and if you don't want to, that's cool. Just think about it."

"I—"

"Come on! Let's get a drink!"

She was dragging him off again. The situation was so cliched: middle-aged workaholic walking arm in arm with a stunning bombshell, feeling like he was real again. It *wasn't* real at all, but that didn't matter.

Their hips bumped as they walked, each bump urging another drop of pre-ejaculant down his urethra. When the tanned skin of her thigh slid against his, he could've moaned.

"I love this bar. Wanna know why?"

"Good drink specials?"

"No! It's outrageously overpriced! But I love it 'cos it's always empty!"

"That's more my speed too," Flood said for lack of an intelligent response.

"I'm supposed to meet my friend Therese here later."

The name crackled in his head. *Therese.* From his eavesdrop on Leon and Jinny. *Jesus, Jinny,* Leon had complained, *you're gonna turn into a junkie like Ann and Therese.* Oxycodone, they'd been talking about: needle-free heroin. But it was clear Carol couldn't be into similar recreations, not with a body and glow like this. She didn't really even look like a prostitute: she looked too grand for that, too perfect.

The bar sprawled before a long, massive swimming pool, before an even more massive pink hotel that looked more like a castle. The elegant edifice threw a football-field sized shadow onto the beach.

No customers at the bar, nor at any of the umbrella'd tables on the bar's flank. This "worked" for Flood, indeed, for at any moment his arousal would be plain to see. An attractive fiftyish woman polished a glass and smiled at them.

"Tequila Moonrise, and whatever my friend's having," Carol said. Flood ordered a Beck's draft.

"And I told you, this is on me," Carol insisted. "I can't afford to eat here, but I can always swing a few drinks."

"I'd be more than happy to p—"

"Hush!"

The drinks arrived. A menu shaped like a scallop shell was placed before them, then the barmaid curtly walked away.

"Wow. Lobster Fritters," Flood commented of the menu. Twenty-two bucks for four.

"They're great but way overpriced. One time I had them, though, and they're delicious. A j—" She stalled. "A client got them for me."

She was going to say a john, Flood realized. "Let's get some. I'm buying. I'm buying everything."

"Jake, come on, I said this was my treat."

"Won't hear of it. And besides—" He looked at her and nearly rolled his eyes in awe. "Where on earth are you carrying money, anyway? I know it's not stashed in that top."

She giggled again, raised her other hand, which brandished

a minuscule fleshtone wrist-purse. She zipped it open and slipped him a business card. "If you're not interested now, maybe you will be later. But just so you know, I'm a grand for all night, and that's anything you want, as many times as you can get off. Five hundred for an hour, and two for a blow. But for you, half off."

Flood looked at the card. Because she'd mentioned Therese after Leon's reference to her, he expected the card to be identical to the one Leon had given him, but instead, this one read: SUN ANGELS TOUR GUIDES - HENRY PHIPPS, MNGR. He remembered the Phipps' name...

Leon's competition...

The side of her calf touched his. She chatted her background, which sounded typical and very non-harrowing. It was small-talk, it was meaningless, and Flood knew that given her profession, *he* was meaningless. He was to her what a potential network buyer was to Flood. Once they said "no, thanks," they were reduced to insignificance. But none of this mattered. She was doing her job with artistry, making him feel at ease and covertly stimulating him with her cheery voice, her giggles, her eye gestures and body language. Flood was enjoying her company, and she hadn't been lying. There was never any pressure. "Those were delicious," she said of the lobster fritters. Flood had also ordered satay, fresh-water shrimp skewers, and lastly, oysters on the half-shell.

"Oh, I love raw oysters. You read my mind!" A hot hand opened on his thigh when she whispered, "And it's true what they say. They really do make me horny!"

Flood smiled. *I'm sure they do. She's working me, all right...and I don't care.*

His breath thinned when he watched her eat, daintily holding up the shell, the tip of her tongue slipping around the oyster. Then she sucked it all right into her mouth.

Oh, God...

And now her gestures became less covert: her hand smoothing over his thigh, her legs rubbing his more directly. "Relax," she whispered next. "She's way over there, and can't see under the bar anyway..."

"What?" Flood began, then gritted his teeth. He tensed when her fingers slipped under his shirt and worked their way into the waistband of his trunks. His balls drew up at once, and even before her hand was on it, his penis shot fully hard. His first social instinct was to pull her hand out—*Someone might see!*—but why care?

"Relax, relax." Her whisper was like hot liquid. "There's no one here. Let me play with it..."

She knew how to play. Her fingers slipped all around, so lightly at first his nerves barely registered the tactility, then with a smooth firmness. Each beat of Flood's heart forced more blood upward, to the extent that his already erect penis seemed to lengthen, by force.

"What do you think?" she whispered.

He could barely talk. "I-can't. You don't understand—it-it won't work. I-I-I can never come. I can never keep it up..."

Her hand gripped the shaft like a flight-stick, the pad of her thumb twirling over the lubricated knob as though his glans were a bomb-release trigger. "Jake, it sure doesn't feel to me like you have any problem." She whispered more hotly, her breath sultry and sweet from the drink. "This is one big hard *cock* I've got here in my hand! Let me take care of it for you. I want to do something for you, you know...for earlier."

His chest felt so tight he could barely breathe. "In a minute, I'll lose it..."

"Yeah?" She didn't sound convinced. She brought her thumb and forefinger together, and slid the ring slowly up and down, the pre-come pouring now. There was so much anyone would have thought his penis had been drenched in baby oil. "Relax, you're just nervous. Look, the barmaid's going back for ice!"

Flood didn't even bother to look.

"I know you're gonna come, I know you are," she insisted. "Get it. Come all over my hand..."

Flood kept his eyes closed. This was another oddity—his erections *never* lasted this long, save for last night during the beating. But there was no beating here, no violence, just perfect, unselfish lust. Perhaps his affliction was wearing off after so many years. *Oh, God, I can only hope...* If the Devil was sitting on the next stool, Flood knew he'd sell his soul just to come.

Her strokes quickened. Flood filled his mind with images of her: her hairless pussy in his face, his cock sliding between the consummate tits. He imagined the taste of her as his tongue spun circles over the clitoral nugget. He could imagine her own tongue cradling the back of each testicle like a spoon cradling an egg.

"Get it, get it. Let it all come out..."

Then the image ruptured. It wasn't his cock anymore on the verge of eruption. It was some other man's. And it was Felicity's hand, not Carol's, and Felicity's voice maintaining the secret whisper, "Get it, get it, *shoot* it..."

Flood's erection died in her hand to total limpness.

She pulled her hand out, perplexed. After some silence, she said, "What happened? Was I doing it wrong?"

"No," his voice crunched like gravel being walked on. He regained his breath, humiliated. "What did you say earlier—your rates, I mean. Was it five hundred for an hour?"

"Yeah, but...I can't charge you anything for *that*. I wouldn't feel right."

At least she's got some real character in there somewhere, he thought. "No, I mean now." He glanced to make sure the barmaid was out of earshot. "I'll give you five hundred right now, just to listen to me. I just want to talk."

Before she could agree, he slipped five bills from his wallet and handed them to her beneath the counter.

"Wow, I—"

It was a lark, Flood knew. But what the hell? The only person he'd ever talked to about this was Dr. Untermann. Back in Seattle, and Seattle was a long way away.

"I want to tell you about this problem I have," he began.

"Okay. Sometimes it's good to talk about a problem with someone you don't know, and someone you'll probably never see again. It feels better afterwards, and sometimes a different perspective helps. An anonymous one. You can talk without worrying about what the other person might think of you."

"Yes," Flood said. "I'm hoping so, anyway. And I'll try not to bore you." Then he began: "I have a sexual dysfunction which my psychiatrist charmingly refers to as a thematic-erotic inversion with ejaculatory incompetence and sequent erectile failure. How's that for a diagnosis?"

"It's a mouthful, all right." She popped a shrimp in her mouth, then whispered, "But they have stuff for that now." Then she held up her wrist purse. "If you need a Viagra, I've got 'em."

"It doesn't work, none of that does." He tapped his temple. "It's all psychological. It's like a toggle-switch in my brain. When I'm with woman, and it gets past a certain point, that sexual switch gets turned off, by a single image, a single memory."

"What memory?"

"My ex-wife. Even after three years, it's like sabotage."

"Do you still love her?"

"Yes, and I know that's ridiculous and illogical. She ruined me—lied, cheated, stole, and left me—but after all that, I know deep down, I'd take her back without thinking twice."

"Why?"

He gave an honest shrug. "Because she was the best sex of my life, and now I can never have that again. My psyche's still obsessed with her; it's not even a conscious thing, at least that's what my therapist has told me. And I believe it. What else can I believe?" Flood's eyes panned over the nearly nude breasts and pubis, all that erotic flesh showing through the net—one of the most erotic images of his life. His penis—and his heart—felt like dead meat. "It's like I'm being haunted," he dragged on, lowering his voice. "It doesn't matter what the circumstance is sexually. Whenever I'm with a woman, right at the moment before I'd...come...I lose my erection, and...no orgasm. As if, right then, right at the moment of *my pleasure,* the woman I'm with becomes my ex-wife, and all that anger and negativity shoots right into my head, and kills all sexual function."

Carol's eyes blinked as she thought. "Okay, so...what about..."

"Masturbation? Same thing. Whatever image is in my head...while I'm doing it—whatever beautiful, stimulating woman— changes into *her*. Felicity."

"Maybe there's something you don't really know about yourself," she suggested. "Have you tried to get it on with guys?"

Flood winced, shaking his head. "No, no, no. I've never been attracted to men, never."

"What about porn?"

"Tried it, doesn't work. Oh, I'll get hard, I'll get excited, but—"

"Right before you'd get off, you lose it."

"Yes," he groaned. His heart had picked up while he'd been telling her, his blood-pressure shooting up. Any reference to Felicity did that, it put him in a state of subdued terror. "Porn, call girls, oils, lubes, herbs, oysters, prescription drugs, even penis-pumps—" He was beginning to blush—"I've tried it all, and it all fails. That toggle gets turned off. Then—nothing."

More contemplation. She'd replaced her hand on his thigh, ran her tongue over her bottom lip as she thought. "Well, now that you've talked about it to someone else, maybe that unplugged the toggle. Let's try..." Her eyes darted off. Now the barmaid was conversing with a bus boy at the other end of the bar, chattering away. Before he could look back to Carol, her face was in his lap, his waistband hauled down. She suckled his balls in her mouth, one at a time, then slipped the deflated penis past her lips. She worked the limp meat like a milking-machine nozzle on a cow teat. When turgidity requited, the action became more dainty, her tongue-tip running slow, excruciating lines up and down the shaft, tracing the veins. She even seemed earnest when she stopped a moment and whispered, "Don't let her come into your head. Think about me," and then she commenced with what he could only guess was the finest act of fellatio ever performed in the history of human sexuality.

His mind felt squashed with images of her, and just when he would fill her mouth with the horrendous back-pressure of sperm—

85

Edward Lee

Felicity fell into his head like a guillotine blade; an instant later, his penis was a tiny and pathetic strip of nerveless meat.

There was nothing to say, yet she smiled just the same and offered, "Jake, whatever this problem is of yours, I know you'll get over it in time."

Flood doubted it but he nodded anyway. He ordered another round of drinks in silence while she patted his thigh in a lost condolence. "And when you *do* get over it," she continued, "find that card, fly back here, and call me."

"I will," he said uselessly. Now it was all gone, any rapport that had been there previously. He drained half his beer in one slug, trying to think of small-talk, but a sudden encroacher saved him:

"Hi, guys!"

An unseen arm was around him, and what felt like a very firm and very large breast pressed against his back.

"Hi, Therese," Carol said.

Flood turned to face a stunning, bright-eyed girl with ember-red hair cut like a flyer's cap. Breasts even larger and more gravity-defying than Carol's gaped back at Flood, jutting from a spritey, lissome pixie. A see-through white sarong and veil flowed off her hips and shoulders—a sun-ghost. Her skin, eyes, and smile radiated a cast of perfect health and vitality. *Sure as hell doesn't look like the prescription-dope junkie Leon was talking about,* Flood surmised. She leaned over and gave Carol a peck on the cheek.

"Therese, this is my friend, Jake. He saved me from the grossest scumbag earlier—yeck! You should've seen this guy. But Jake whipped his ass."

"Defender of Women!" Therese exclaimed, then it was Jake's cheek that got pecked.

This is fucking killing me, Flood thought.

Therese was petite and short, and would've been shorter were it not for the heavily-soled beach sandals that elevated her. She lowered her face between the two of them, grinned impishly. "So are we doing a threeway, or what? I'm so horny I'm starting to show through my thong! Look, Jake—" and she squeezed next to him and pulled her thong down beneath

86

the bartop. Flood's eyes roved down the flat belly to see that what she revealed: an adorable little toy of a pussy, dusted by the lightest red fur. The meticulous cleft below glistened.

"She's such a bad girl, Jake—and I mean sometimes she's *really* bad," Carol giggled. Then, to Therese: "Put that away!"

Both girls laughed; Therese repositioned the thong, then patted the adhesive triangle of fabric.

Flood ordered another round of drinks, testicles tingly. *Yes. This is definitely fucking killing me...*

"Jake and I just did some business," Carol sort of lied. "Now we're just talking."

"Oh. That's cool. Sorry I missed the fun. Maybe next time?" She gave Flood's tortured crotch a finger-tickling squeeze.

"Sure," Flood answered and drank more.

He was grateful that the next few minutes of banter didn't regard any manner of sex—just enlivened chit-chat. He *wasn't* necessarily grateful for Carol's hand on one thigh and Therese's on the other. Flood slowly grew erect again, painstakingly so, and at this point—the futility of it all now burying him as if in a hole—he felt as though an abstract bullet had been put through his head. Flood was the diabetic working in the Godiva chocolate factory; the Olympic swimmer standing in the middle of the Sahara Desert. So he drank gluttonously, pretending to listen to the girls' chat but hoping that enough alcohol would deaden his sexual nerves.

"Well, I better get going now," Carol said. "Thanks for everything, Jake. It was great hanging out with you."

Flood took a last useless look at the perfect breasts suspended in the big fishnet cups. "Likewise."

Therese gave his thigh another squeeze. "Where are you staying, Jake?"

"The Rosamilia Hotel, just up the beach."

Her breasts jiggled flawlessly when she stood up. "Cool. That's where I'm staying too."

"Maybe we'll run into you before you leave," Carol offered.

Flood was done talking, done thinking, and very much *done* with seeing what he couldn't have. "That'd be great," he said for formality. "You girls have a great day."

"'Bye."

"'Bye!"

Two more pecks on the cheek (and a final insufferable crotch-rub from Therese), and they were off. It was relief from the humiliation that overwhelmed Flood when they left. Their shadows lengthened to sultry jet-black threads as they departed back to the sand.

His head droned with an arid silence, noise that wasn't noise. The sound of his soul? Because that's what his soul felt like just then. Arid, sterile. A husk.

It occurred to him that if he died at that very moment...he wouldn't have cared in the least.

His hangover dragged through the dinner hour and on into the night. He didn't bother checking in with Farris and Nathans to see how the day's business went; he didn't care. He lay naked and dried out on the hotel bed, head thumping, sparks of pain behind his eyes, throbbing along with the images of those two impeccable women: the abundant flesh of Carol's breasts blaring through the fishnets, the sparse mist of downy red hair covering Therese's mound. The coltish legs and flat abdomens. Each image twinged in his head with his heartbeat, and each heartbeat made him feel more hopeless. He thought of calling Dr. Untermann and telling her he felt like maybe committing suicide but didn't for two reasons.

One: *She'd think I was even more pathetic than I really am.*

And, two: *I don't have the balls.*

The sun had set brilliantly—a fireball that looked nuclear—and soon full dark bled into the room. Flood stared at the ceiling, not listening to the baseball game that shot scatters of wavering light on one wall. He wished he could fall asleep, erase the humiliating day, and begin a new man in the morning.

But he *wouldn't* be a new man, would he?

He'd be the same impotent, royally-fucked-up-in-the-head man he was today and had been for the last three years.

As his senses began to drift, he heard voices...

"It ain't bad really, we're doing better than the rest. We got fifteen girls and only a handful went bad. I'm sure Jinny won't fuck us over again. I think the skinny bitch learned her lesson."

Flood sat up in bed, glanced to his window. It was Oscar's voice, the big bad bald guy. *I left the window open,* Flood realized. The curtains billowed at a breeze. And the maids hadn't come in because he'd left out the do-not-disturb sign.

Flood sprang out of bed, seized, but not exactly knowing why. Just as he arrived to the window's edge, Leon's voice was floating up.

"I know. You're one terrifying motherfucker, Osc. Jinny'll have nightmares about you." A laugh.

"Bitch sucked my balls the whole time I was driving her home, then begged me to fuck her in the ass back at her joint."

A darker resolve shifted into Leon's next words. "But the other two are liabilities."

The other two? Flood recited.

"I had dinner with Therese tonight. Cunt lied to my face all through her steak. Got no idea Stoolie's ratting on Phipps' stable."

"You're shitting me?"

"Nope."

A pause drifted in with the warm breeze. Oscar said, "Lemme kill her. I've always hated the bitch."

Flood's heart stilled. He felt frozen, half his face peering out his window down into the window of Room 415. He could see the salmon-pink drapes fluttering, and in their gap, the brightly lit room. Oscar sat on the bed drinking a Heineken; Flood could see his knees and back of his large, shaven head. Leon sat in the chair along the wall, legs crossed.

"I don't want her iced, but I want her uglied up bad for when we boot her lying ass back to Phipps."

The back of Oscar's bald head nodded.

"It's that other lying cunt I want iced," Leon added.

"Good. It'd be a pleasure."

Now Flood's heart surged, a lump of muscle that felt on the verge of bursting. The other one? *No!* he thought. *Not Carol!*

Who was the *other* one?

"I'm not sure where she is tonight," Leon continued. "I already talked to Nick. He's going to keep an eye out for her."

"Nick? Oh, yeah, the new security guy downstairs."

"I'm paying him well. He'll give me a call on my cell if he sees her."

WHO ARE THEY TALKING ABOUT? Flood's mind detonated.

But Carol had given him his card; she worked directly for Phipps, not Leon. *If she was two-timing on Leon, she'd have Leon's card, wouldn't she?* he reasoned.

It didn't matter. Nothing would happen to either girl because Flood was going to make an anonymous tip to the police right now. Last night was a mistake, a weakness on his part.

And that won't happen again, he vowed.

It amazed him how the sound from their window carried so well up here. He could even hear the knock on their door.

"That's her," Leon said.

Oscar got up and walked out of the frame.

Flood stood shivering. He watched, unblinking, as Therese walked into a corner of the window. "Hi, guys!" she greeted. "Got a beer or something?"

Oscar handed her one.

"And I'll need a oxy for later."

"No problem, babe."

"Oh, and look!" she exclaimed, all bouncy and bubbling and probably really high. She shoved some money at Leon. "Four hundred!"

"Thank you, Therese. You're a dear."

Flood could see her in the veil-like wrap she'd been wearing at the bar, her sleek back to the window, her short, bright-scarlet hair. Her rump looked naked due to the t-back, a perfect double-orb of flesh.

"I got some time," she said, but she seemed jittery now, overstrung. Was it the dope, or was she starting to think something might be wrong? "Got two doctors said they'll meet me at midnight for a double blowjob, said they'd pay five bills. You guys wanna fuck me first? I'm dying for some cock." A giggle, then, that sounded nervous. "I been so horny all day I been fingering myself whenever I've been sitting at a table."

"Yeah, I could use some of that," Leon said.

She shed the veil, then flicked off the t-back and bra. It seemed so perfunctory when she turned for the bed, but an instant later her breasts were suddenly tremoring. Her eyes bulged above Leon's opened hand, which had snapped around and clamped over her mouth. "Not too hard," Leon said very calmly. "Just put her lights out..."

WHAP!

Oscar, having already slipped on one of the sand-mitts, clouted her solidly once in the forehead. She fell limp as a sack of packing peanuts in Leon's arms. He tossed her on the bed—

—while Flood...watched.

His hand remained poised in mid-air—just like last night—about to reach for the phone. But instead—

Call. The. Police...

—he watched.

Oscar wrapped some duct tape around her mouth, then dropped his slacks and straddled her chest. She lay totally unconscious, arms and legs askew, head lolled to one side. Oscar spat liberally into the valley, then pressed the breasts tight around his penis and began to pump. Meanwhile, Leon had picked up one of Therese's inch-soled platform sandals, was fidgeting with it. "There we go, Osc," he said. He found some sort of clasp on the bottom of the sandal, then was peeling back the sole. "Stoolie wasn't jiving us."

"For the money you pay him to be our squeal, why would he?"

91

Inside the sandal there was some sort of a compartment, from which Leon withdrew a roll of cash. "Damn it, Osc. Bitch was hiding twelve hundred bucks in here. *My* money."

Oscar humped the slick crevice between Therese's bulging breasts, his hairy ass pistoning back and forth with the precision of a derrick. "And she was gonna leave here tomorrow and give it all to that white nigger Henry Phipps."

Leon was not offended by the "n"-word. "This shit hurts, man. I treat these girls right. What is it about that goddamn Phipps that has my bitches handin' him their money like he's Snoop Dog and Tupac combined?"

Oscar's answer was forestalled for his orgasm, which looped into Therese's still face. When he began talking again, he was wringing the last of it out of his cock like water out of a dishrag. "It ain't him, Leon. Wanna know what it is?"

"Tell me, my man."

"It's you. You're too nice to these bitches. You *let 'em* walk on you. If there's a buck to be made, these girls'll eat cum out of an ass-crack like a kid eating icing off a cupcake. Only thing white-trash like this respects is a Mack-Daddy who means business, a hard fuckin' hand, man."

"You know, Osc? You're right. It don't make sense, but you're right. And this is one hand that's gonna get real hard real fast. But it just hurts, ya know?"

"Don't worry about it." Oscar was pulling his pants back up. "It ain't no big deal in the long run anyway. Any crew's gotta couple bad girls. We're weeding ours out." Oscar paused, extended a hand to the still-unconscious Therese. "You wanna piece of this before I start working on her?"

"No. She disgusts me."

And the entire scene disgusted Flood. He watched from his secret vantage point, hand still in the air to pick up the phone. His most sophisticated human senses felt severed, leaving only a blazing, mindless lust. His penis throbbed so hard it hurt, erect now beyond any maximum he'd ever experienced. Only the barest filament left of his spirit remained bellowing at him to call the police as, below, Oscar re-donned his sand-mitt and re-straddled Therese's chest.

"Remember, don't kill her," Leon instructed. "But I want that pretty little face of hers fucked up royally. When Phipps takes his first look at her, I want him to puke."

WHAP! came the first blow, which most certainly crushed her nose. Four more to either side just as certainly shattered her cheekbones and jaw. In only a matter of seconds, her face more resembled a stepped-on jelly donut than a human visage.

It was as though Flood's skin had been nailed to the wall and he was pulling that skin through the nailheads when he finally managed to drag himself away from the window to the desk with the phone. Only three steps but in those three steps the hardest erection of his life went utterly limp.

Then that last filament of humanity made its exit.

If anything, his cock grew even harder when he stepped back to the window, a tethered animal with rabies, just about to break its chain. Flood knew then that he had no choice at this point...

He was masturbating at the window, sweat pouring. Oscar had already popped Therese hard over each eye, turning them to blue-black puffs of flesh. And now—

WHAP! WHAP! WHAP!

He was belly-punching her, his stout arm piledriving straight down with each blow. Bulbous breasts jounced with each slug.

Flood's climax burst, releasing the mental stopper on the day's agonizing back-up of semen. Like last night, it flew out the window in what seemed several yard-long strings. And like last night, there'd been not an inkling of any last-second sabotaging image of Felicity. His orgasm unwound as a celebration, bringing tears to his eyes. He staggered back when it was finally all gone, his loins buzzing. His cock felt content as a beast that had just fed gluttonously.

When he regained some order of sense, he found himself looking back down.

Please, God. Let them be done...

Oscar and Leon *weren't* done.

The bald man hunkered low, in one hand an empty beer bottle, in the other a hammer.

"You said you wanted her fucked up. Well, *this'll* fuck her up."

Leon stood, a knuckle to his lips, contemplating. "No, no—"

"What? Going back to Mr. Nice Guy?"

"She could bleed to death, Osc. I don't want that. I know— Do like you did that one chick we had a couple years ago. Remember? That Gothy looking bitch who was trying to hustle our girls for some service in Key West."

"Oh, yeah! Balloon Pussy! Straight up." Oscar put the bottle and hammer away, then put the mitt back on. He pushed Therese's ankles back toward her head, where Leon then grabbed them and pulled them back further. Her ass spread; the flesh of her vagina bloomed forward.

Oscar slapped down hard against her bared loins with the mitt's open palm. Time and time again, as hard as a strong man could. Flood reeled, nauseated, but locked in place by the taunt of an instantaneous erection as turgid and insistent as the one his hand had relieved a minute ago. He squeezed it; it felt hard as a steel-tube covered with skin, lust and blood purpling its dome, the slit inflamed and glazed already.

Oh my God...

Again, that blade severed his humanity. Now Oscar was punching down outright into Therese's sex, which was blacking and bluing and swelling before his eyes.

WHAP! WHAP! WHAP! WHAP! WHAP! WHAP!

And more.

"Lookit that," Oscar remarked, subtly impressed by the image of his handiwork. The majoras of Therese's vagina, indeed, had ballooned with swelling, and with that image the pressure of desire built up similarly in Flood's penis, backed by further semen straining to be released. Flood thought of a water balloon being slowly squeezed. The idea of calling the police, now, did not exist anywhere in his head. Flood masturbated frenetically, eyes locked below.

Oscar and Leon were chuckling at the image of Therese's ludicrously swollen sex.

"I can't help it, man," Oscar chuckled further, dropping

his slacks again. "I've just *gotta* fuck this..."

Oscar banged away, for quite awhile, as Flood nearly jerked the skin off of his own cock. At the moment when he would normally lose everything—when the image of Therese would invert to Felicity—Flood bit down on his lip to stifle the shriek of his pleasure that surely would've echoed outside. The first spurt blew against the glass, several more landed in loops on the carpet. This second orgasm of the night felt heroin-like. He stood ridiculously, heart hammering, legs still spread and one arm bracing him against the window frame. Insensible, he looked down and saw an impossibly still-hard penis throbbing. The final string of semen dangled from the piss-slit. When he squeezed his balls, the erection involuntarily flexed, and hook-shotted the remaining sperm in an upward arch where it stuck to his chest like a piece of flung spaghetti.

"Not enough," Leon said, out of frame. "It's the tits that bother me now."

"What about 'em?" Oscar was pulling his pants up again, while Therese lay with her legs wishboned, her genitals a dark swell. "That's the best pair of tits in your stable."

Leon kept the contemplative finger to his lips. "Yeah, and that's the problem. I *paid* for them. Let Henry Phipps pay for the next pair."

"Sounds fair to me," Oscar chuckled and produced an ice pick.

Flood couldn't move, paralyzed by the combinant disgust of continuing to watch while his loins still buzzed in post-orgasm.

Oscar had obviously done work like this before. Under each of Therese's breasts, he quickly shivved the ice pick up several times, puncturing the implants. Then he lifted his leg and stepped on each breast, deflating them. Multiple streams of red-tinted saline sprayed down Therese's lower body. A minute later, her state-of-the-art breasts were popped bags of skin.

"Much better," Leon said. "Let Phipps titty-fuck *that...*"

That was it for Flood. He almost lost his footing then,

heels thumping backward until his knees gave out against the edge of the bed. Then he fell over on the mattress.

And lay there perfectly still.

He couldn't have gotten up again if he'd wanted to. But he could still hear them talking, ghost-voices fluttering around in the dark.

Leon: "Oh, yeah, that's a good job. This lying bitch is *hosed*."

"Lemme get her ready."

"Right. I'll go down to the parking garage and bring the van around to the security door. I'll also have Nick come up and help you get her down the stairs. He'll lock all the stairwell doors on each floor so you can get her down without anyone seeing."

"Got'cha. That was fun. Wish we could be there when Phipps takes a look at what's lyin' in his driveway in the morning."

Flood's heart felt truly dead.

"And it's a shame, too. Greed is what I mean. And the other one's worse. Taking a commission on any girl of mine she can swing over to Phipps. I can't be embarrassed like this, I can't have it. I can't have that gold-toothed piece of cracker shit laughing at me."

"You're talking about Ann now, ain't you?"

"Yes. You know what we have to do, right?"

"Sure."

"You have any problem with that?"

A chuckle. "Me? I groove on it."

"Excellent. Tomorrow, then. You pound that whore's face in till she's dead."

"Oh, Mr. Flood, our records show that you're booked for another night," the lanky hotel clerk observed at the desk.

"Yes," Flood mumbled. "Something came up; I've gotta leave a day early."

"Oh, okay. I hope you enjoyed your stay at the Rosamilia." The clerk produced a receipt, then Flood made a quick exit through the revolving door to the sun-lit entrance circle.

He couldn't leave till tomorrow, but there was no way he'd be staying the last night here. The place disgusted him, because it reminded him of what he'd done—or what he *hadn't* done—while Therese was being raped, beaten, and mutilated. It reminded him of what an utterly irredeemable human being he was...

The wheels of his suitcase squealed as he walked over to the next hotel. He knew what he *would* do, though; he simply hadn't done it yet and wasn't quite sure why. *Haven't worked up the nerve,* he supposed. *A coward all ways...* The procrastination, at least, gave him time for some lame rationalization. *I couldn't have called the police last night, because the call could be traced back to my room. Couldn't call from my cell phone, either—it's gotta be anonymous. And I couldn't call security 'cos that'd be even worse. Leon's got the hotel security man on his payroll.*

It worked a little, at least.

I'll call the police from a pay phone, blow the whistle on the shit going on in Room 415. I'll tell the cops about Jinny and Therese. Leon and Oscar will get questioned and spooked, not knowing who ratted on them. Maybe Jinny and Therese will even decide to press charges once the cat's out of the bag. I'll call Henry Phipps, too, from the card Carol gave me. The cops'll put major heat on everybody, and at the very least, Leon and Oscar won't beat up anymore girls, and they sure as shit won't be killing this other girl tonight.

Flood sighed.

Then I'll go back to Seattle and forget I ever came to this awful beach...

He stowed his bags at the new hotel, then made it over to the convention center. Nathans and Farris were exuberant; Flood had his sign-up meetings with a flock of corporate buyers, and deals were sealed. It took the rest of the afternoon but to Flood, with all that guilt sitting on his shoulder, each meeting went by in a fog. By dinnertime, he was done, and when he went back out to the showroom, his associates were high-fiving each other.

"This has to be our biggest haul at a con," Nathans was

rubbing his hands together.

"You might be right," Flood said.

"We're making the west coast sales dickheads look like doodly-squat," Farris added.

"Can't disagree with that, either," Flood said. "You guys did great."

"Great enough for a night on the town—on the company account?" Nathans pushed it.

"Once you guys get everything packed up..." Flood gave him a company credit card, "yeah. Have a good time."

"Thanks, boss! Won't you be joining us?"

"No, can't. But I'll see you guys at the airport in the morning."

"Come on," Farris implored. "We'll hit some of those kick-ass strip joints in Tampa."

The idea deadened the little left of Flood's soul. "No, count me out, guys."

"He must have a hot date." Nathans grinned.

"Nope," Flood assured. "But I've got a very important call to make."

Flood left them in the convention's decaying buzz. He knew what he had to do, and he knew he *was* going to do it this time. The anonymity of the call would guarantee his protection; there'd be no way Leon or Oscar could come calling for him because they'd have no idea who made the call. The police would have to follow up on something this severe...

The phone coves were all full, sellers either reporting windfall sales to their home-bases, or a dismal turnout. Flood wasn't thwarted; he simply crossed the street back to the Rosamilia but when he found their phone cove full too, he saw no harm in putting off the call a while longer for some dinner.

He ate light and tried to relax, feeling better at least for knowing that he would soon report Leon's crimes, however late. He couldn't blame himself entirely, could he? Getting beaten up by your pimp was a hazard of any prostitute's calling.

Flood even recognized that these mental observations were indeed excuses, but that was okay now because he was going to stop it all.

And the time is now...

He left the restaurant and went straight to the phone cove where there were plenty of available phones. He sat in the first booth, lit a cigarette in spite of the NO SMOKING sign, and took some time to think. *And there's another girl named Ann,* he could tell the police. *When they find her, they're going to kill her.* Then he'd hang up and leave.

Easy.

But before he could dial, another voice leaked in through the gap in the booth's folding door, a woman's.

"Hey, Jimmy, this is Ann. Remember me? Yeah, yeah, two nights ago at the Swigwam. You said I could give you a call. Still game for tonight?"

Flood sat frozen, listening.

Ann...

Something moved then at the fringes of his vision. He didn't quite catch it.

Figures entering the cove?

A tap, not at his door but at the next.

"Okay, Jimmy, look, lemme call you back in a few, okay? Something just came up." A girlish chuckle. "Yeah, yeah, that too. Talk to ya real soon—'bye."

"There she is," a man's voice could be heard.

Another man's: "We've been looking all over for you, we were worried."

"I told you I'd be here, Leon. And here I am."

Leon and obviously Oscar.

"Good," Leon said. "I got a rich as hell optometrist wanting you in a bad way, showed him your pic in the brochure. But he's only got an hour, and his wife's in his room."

"That's cool. How about I use your room?"

"Great. Here're the keys. Go get ready, and we'll bring him up. He's going to meet us in the bar in a few minutes."

"Sure thing. I'll call you on your cell when he's done." Then the door in the next booth closed, and a woman walked by.

Flood's mouth locked open.

It was Carol.

She sauntered by, jingling keys in her hand.

When she was gone, the men talked further.

Oscar: "She ain't on to us."

"Yeah, the bitch is so arrogant, thinks she can get over on anyone."

"Never even knew her real name was Ann. Guess that's what she goes by when she's working behind my back for Phipps. Ain't that some shit?"

"Yeah, well. She's got a new name now: dead meat."

"Let's have a drink in the bar, then go up."

"Fine by me. Man, I can't wait to punch this bitch's ticket..."

Still as a stone, Flood remained in the booth. Leon and Oscar walked out of the cove.

They're going to do it, Flood's thoughts grated like ratchets. *They're going to be killing Carol in a few minutes...*

The phone felt melted in his hand. The numbers on the buttons blurred in his vision, and as his shaking index finger trembled forward, a sound like distant turbine filled his head.

Wait a minute...

Flood never dialed. He got a better idea instead. He left the phone hanging and walked out of the booth. A spit-and-polish concierge smiled stiffly when Flood approached. "How may I be of service, sir?"

"Where's the nearest Bank of America? I've got an emergency."

The concierge pointed toward the front. "There's one right across the street..."

Flood stared at the metal numbers: 415.

He gulped once, then knocked.

The low voices inside ceased when his knuckles rapped against the door. *Leon's probably looking through the peephole right now,* Flood deduced with a scared smile. He didn't give a shit anymore. He knocked again, then held his cell phone up before the peephole. "Open up or I'm calling the cops..."

The door to Room 415 clicked, then yawned open.

Flood wasn't surprised when he stepped in and found Oscar's pistol to his head. "Easy, pal. I've got business to discuss. And don't shit a brick. I know you're about to kill the girl."

Oscar glared in silent rage, his bald pate nearly quivering. He shoved Flood into the main room where Leon stood.

"He says he knows about Carol," Oscar said. "What the fuck's going on?"

Leon gaped at Flood. "You..."

Flood surrendered his cell phone to Oscar, then nodded to Leon. "You remember me. From the elevator?"

"Jack... Flood?"

"Makes sense you'd remember faces and names, you being a pimp and all—"

Leon was aghast. "Oscar, who *is* this guy? Why is he here?"

"I'm here to talk business," Flood began, smiling in spite of an effusion of sweat. "Of course, you guys can kill me right now, and no one would know."

"Oh, we can kill you, all right," Oscar began.

"Right, and you'd be stupid, which is par for the course so far." Flood noticed a closed door behind them. *That's the bedroom...* "First of all, you guys talk way too loud. I overheard several of your conversations in the phone cove downstairs." He pointed to the closed door. "And there's a couple-inch gap between those pink curtains in there. You both are about as sharp as Oscar's head."

Leon and Oscar remained stiff where they stood.

"I saw you beat up Jinny two nights ago," Flood finished. "And I saw what you did to Therese last night. You guys really take the cake for sick motherfuckers."

Leon's eyes bloomed toward Oscar. "I don't believe this shit, Oscar. What are we gonna do with this guy?"

"I got a couple ideas," Oscar said.

"Yeah, yeah," Flood chuckled. It was beyond him how he could be keeping his cool amid these killers. "Look, I know you got Carol in the bedroom—er, I guess her real name's Ann. I'd like to see her. What's the big deal? You guys got a gun on me. Let's go in there and talk business."

Leon's face remained stamped with disbelief. He nodded to Oscar, then they escorted Flood into the room.

Carol lay stretched naked over a shower curtain covering the bed, her ankles and wrists tied to the posts. Her eyes bugged above her gag. *God, she's beautiful,* Flood thought. The rotund, perfect implants quivered, her flat stomach sucking in and out in terror. Flood quailed when he noted the sand-mitts on the dresser, along with a cord and tourniquet, a manual drill, and a soldering iron.

Flood reserved comment. Instead he pointed to the gap in the salmon curtains. "See. At just the right angle, you can see in from outside."

"Bullshit," Leon muttered. "There ain't nothin' but the Gulf of fuckin' Mexico out there," but then he peeked out and up.

"The end-wing of the building," Floor said. "I was on the fifth floor. It was a million-to-one that the bed, the gap, and the vantage point all added up."

"Shit," Leon muttered and closed the curtains. He rubbed his face. "I still don't know what the fuck's going on. I can't *believe* this."

Flood chuckled again. "And I can't *believe* that Oscar hasn't frisked me yet. Shame on you, Osc. You're the bulldog, right? You're Leon's lieutenant. It's your job to protect The Man."

Oscar slammed Flood belly to wall and began to pat him down.

"Right and left jacket pockets, Osc..."

Oscar's face gaped like a kissing fish when he extracted five bands of $100 bills. "Holy fuck, Leon. There's a lot of fuckin' money here..."

"Fifty grand, Oscar," Flood told him. "I just got it out of the bank. It's for you guys."

Silence brewed like broth while Leon counted the money. His eyes seemed alight against the dark, shiny face. "Mr. Flood? To what do we own this excess of generosity?"

Without asking, Flood lit a cigarette while he tried to tame the nervous tremor in his hands. "I'm buying the girl," came his blunt reply. "Ann."

Leon was shaking his head. "Mr. Flood? This is quite unusual."

"Yeah," Oscar agreed.

"And I sense that you're a smart man..."

I'm a fucked up man, Flood almost chuckled. *Not necessarily a smart one.* "So are you, I hope. I think that handing fifty grand in cash over to you guys is proof of my good faith—"

Leon opened his mouth to talk but Flood cut him off.

"Let me have my say first, Leon, because you and I both know I could be dead a minute from now. You can keep the fifty grand and let the girl go, or..." Flood looked to Oscar. "Care to finish the sentence, Osc?"

Oscar smirked. "Or we can keep the fifty grand, kill the girl and kill you."

"Bingo," Flood said. "And you're thinking if you let her go, she'll go to the cops but, really guys, there's no evidence that any crimes have been committed here. She's a junkie and a prostitute. If you let her walk out that door, the only place she's gonna go is straight to the bus station. She'd be too afraid of you guys coming after her later." Flood turned his gaze. "Right, Leon?"

Leon looked back at him deadpan.

"And if you kill her *and* me," Flood continued, "you guys will never get the *other* fifty grand."

More silence stretched over the room. "What *other* fifty grand might this be?" Leon asked, tapping his Gucci'd foot.

Flood dragged his cigarette deep. "The other fifty grand I give you after the girl is out of here."

Oscar stepped forward. "It's on you?"

"Of course not, Einstein."

Oscar seemed duped by the remark. "Who's Ein—"

"Shut up, Oscar," Leon cut in. "Mr. Flood's got this thought out pretty well."

Flood chuckled out loud. "At least I hope so. Let the girl

go, Leon. You've got nothing to lose."

Leon stroked his chin. "And fifty grand to gain, you say..."

"Right. How can I be bullshitting when I just handed you the first fifty?"

Leon sat down. The silk slacks hissed when he crossed his legs.

"I don't know about this, Leon," Oscar said.

Leon looked straight ahead when he said, "Oscar. Let her go."

Oscar's brow accordioned when he broke from his stance and cast a glance at Flood. He went to the bed then, and begrudgingly untied Carol aka Ann.

"You just won the lottery, cunt," he informed her.

The girl was vibrating when she faltered off the bed and pulled on her clothes. She'd obviously urinated, and all her skin looked pasty with fear-sweat. She stepped forward, then looked at Leon.

"Leave town," Leon said to her. "Mr. Flood here is correct. One way or another, one of my people will find you..."

The girl's hands shook so fiercely she could barely get her dress back on. Her lower lip trembled. For an irreducible moment, she glanced to Flood...

Flood saw noting but a wasteland in her eyes.

She grabbed her wrist-purse and scampered out of the room.

"Ain't that just like a bitch?" Oscar cracked a laugh, then slapped Flood hard on the back. "Didn't even say thank you!"

"It's my karma," Flood said through a thin smile.

But Leon wasn't smiling. He pressed his hands together and rested his chin on his fingertips, looking at Flood.

"Well, Mr. Flood? When will you enlighten us about this *other* fifty thousand?"

Flood lit another cigarette. "As soon as you guys finish packing..."

***

Flood sat in the seedy bathroom, the lights off. He'd left the door open a crack, which afforded him a perfect view of the bed. He arranged an ash tray on the rim of the filmy bathtub, and was actually sitting on the toilet seat lid.

Classy, he joked to himself.

The five-hour flight had passed like a barely recalled dream. The only reason Flood knew about the A-Top motel on Aurora Avenue was due to the time he'd had to stay there overnight when a mudslide had blocked the highway from the Seattle airport. There were no better rooms to book unless he wanted to drive all the way back to Sea-Tac. It was the kind of place that had cockroaches but at least the cockroaches were dead. $59.99 per night and very remote. The parking lot was near empty, and Flood had deliberately booked the farthest room in the complex, so they could park in back

He watched through the door crack, smoking. Leon sat cross-legged on a rickety chair; he was counting the second cash payment. The TV was turned on, the sound turned down: a baseball game.

At the airport, Flood had rented an SUV for Oscar. Then he drove Leon and himself to the motel in his Cadillac Seville.

Risk, he thought baldly. Now that he'd given them the rest of the money... *They could still kill me.* Certainly. But Flood didn't think they would.

The sand-mitts lay on the dresser, along with a cord and tourniquet, a manual drill, and a soldering iron, plus pliers, a fileting knife, and some razor blades...

Maybe I'm just like them, Flood suspected. *Or maybe I'm far worse...*

That's when Oscar entered, with a very unconscious Felicity slung over his shoulder.

"No one saw a thing," the bald man bragged. "I had her snatched two seconds after she came out of the house..."

"Good work," Leon said.

Flood couldn't hear anything save for the drone in his head, when he stood up in the dark and lowered his trousers. His penis was so hard it hurt.

"Let's get her tied down to the bed, and make sure the gag's tight," Leon advised. "Then wake her up and get to work."

Oscar chuckled, eyeing the implements on the nightstand. He plugged in the soldering gun.

Flood broke out in a sweat when he watched them strip the clothes off his ex-wife and lash her spread-eagled on the bed. His ecstacy made his blood seem scalding.

Flood had a feeling his cure was at hand.

Author's Afterword: I got the idea for the "Room 415" story one night while standing in a dark hotel room at about 4 a.m. This was four or five years ago. I'd taken a trusty Greyhound to Orlando in order to attend a Florida-writers book signing, and then I drank too many beers at an industrial club called Independent where publisher Dave Barnett moonlights as a DJ and enjoys the Life of Riley. I had a blast, even after realizing that I was twenty years older than almost everyone in the club, after which Dave treated me and others in his posse to a preeminently grease-laden breakfast at a seedy all-night diner. When I got back to my hotel room—Room 415—I discovered to my horror that it was a non-smoking room. So I did what all respectable smokers do in a non-smoking room. I smoked. I turned out all the lights and stood brazenly in my shorts before the window, which I opened as far as it would go (only a couple of inches. A "governor" was installed, presumably to thwart jumpers. Neat.) So I'm standing there smoking, at this wee hour, in the dark, when I look down and notice a window lit in a room one floor below and caddy-cornered against my vantage point. A several-inch gap existed between the salmon-colored curtains, and in the gap I could see a bed. And that's it.

I need to assure you all that the aforementioned is the ONLY aspect of this story rooted in truth. But as I was standing there watching my smoke siphon out my window, and periodically glancing down to the caddy-cornered window, Hitchcock's REAR WINDOW came to mind. "What if I saw someone get murdered in that window, right now?" I asked myself. "And what if it was a beautiful nude woman?" (Nudity seems to be an auxiliary ornament in most of my work.) Anyway, then I went to bed and awoke with a stunning hangover, and while Greyhounding back home the next day, all the details of the story were already in my head, with pretty much no conscious effort.

Very recently I read a Stephen King quote (in, I believe, the Cindy Margolis issue of Playboy—hubba-hubba) where King cited that he often gets story ideas simply from seeing a particular thing, after which the plot begins to create itself in his head. Though Mr. King's bank account and acclaim have precious little in common with mine, I was enthused to discover this singular commonality: I regularly get entire story ideas that originated by my witnessing some "thing." House, car, road, person, sound, etc. or some other essentially non-descript thingamajig that for some reason fires a subconscious creative spark. Most of the flesh in my novel THE BACKWOODS, for instance, was rooted in my glimpsing a 17-year locust through the window of a cab taking me to BWI airport in Maryland. A house right across the street from my wonderfully squalid apartment proved the initial fuel for FLESH GOTHIC (because the house is actually an office for a porno company. I live in a classy town.) The major plot device in the novella MINOTAURESS (a prequel to THE HORN-CRANKER) was incited decades ago when I was a security guard inspecting an unoccupied two story house. I was checking the locks of this supposedly untenanted dwelling when I heard a toilet flush upstairs. Ooo. Creepy. After possibly peeing my security pants in terror, I envisioned a monster sitting on the upstairs toilet. (The flusher, I'm happy to say, wasn't a monster, it was another security guard I didn't know was inside.) And in the case of this story—"Room 415"—it was something as simple as a hotel window that would hand me the entire plot and character line. This is my reason for cringing when asked that most cliched question: "Where do you get your ideas?" It takes too damn long to explain and is actually quite unremarkable.

Afterwords are often unnecessary, and even more often boring, yet due to a publishing intricacy, I feel the situation warrants a tad more verbosity from Edward Lee. When Necro Publications began production on their excellent DAMNED Anthology, the publisher teamed up with Tampa's Camelot Books to jointly produce a super-fancy (and super pricey) "deluxe" edition for hardcore collectors. Only thirteen copies of this deluxe edition would be sold, and to enhance its uniqueness, I was contracted to write a story that would be exclusive to that edition. The story was "Room 415," but with a condition: that I could publish an alternate version later. When I was writing the piece, two different endings immediately occurred to me. One ending—a longer one—was what I'd call more commercial yet very negative, while the other ending was downright nihilistic. The latter ending wound up being the one I wrote for the deluxe inclusion. My favorite ending, however, is the one you've read. While it's by no means a "happy" ending, it's not as dark and soul-dead as the deluxe. Why, then, is this my favorite? I think because I may be turning into a candyass as I get older. A wimp, but a happy wimp no less.

So. It seems that I've just penned about a thousand words to explain what would've sufficed with two sentences. Ah, the economy of language, and the disciplined skill of the true artist! I'm nearing the three-million-published-words point in my jubilant and unseemly career so, really, what's an extra thousand? This only to assure those thirteen hardcore souls who laid down serious coin that the version of "Room 415" in their deluxe does indeed remain exclusive. And as for those of you who've purchased this version, thank you. It's a story I like very much, and I hope you did to.

ABOUT THE AUTHOR

Edward Lee has authored close to 50 books in the field of horror; he specializes in hardcore fare. His most recent novels are LUCIFER'S LOTTERY and the Lovecraftian THE HAUNTER OF THE THRESHOLD. His movie HEADER was released on DVD by Synapse Film in June, 2009. Lee lives in Largo, Florida.

deadite press

"Brain Cheese Buffet" Edward Lee - collecting nine of Lee's most sought after tales of violence and body fluids. Featuring the Stoker nominated "Mr. Torso," the legendary gross-out piece "The Dritiphilist," the notorious "The McCrath Model SS40-C, Series S," and six more stories to test your gag reflex.
"Edward Lee's writing is fast and mean as a chain saw revved to full-tilt boogie."
    - Jack Ketchum

"Bullet Through Your Face" Edward Lee - No writer is more extreme, perverted, or gross than Edward Lee. His world is one of psychopathic redneck rapists, sex addicted demons, and semen stealing aliens. Brace yourself, the king of splatterspunk is guaranteed to shock, offend, and make you laugh until you vomit.
"Lee pulls no punches."
    - Fangoria

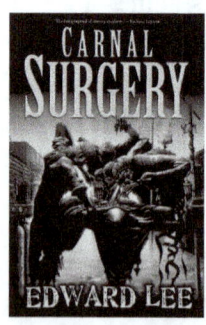

"Carnal Surgery" Edward Lee - Autopsy fetishes, crippled sex slaves, a serial killer who keeps the hands of his victims, government conspiracies, dead cops and doomed pornographers. From operating room morality plays to a town that serves up piss and cum mixed drinks, this is the strange and disturbing world of Edward Lee. From one of the most notorious, controversial, and extreme voices in horror fiction comes a new collection of depravity and terror. Carnal Surgery collects eleven of Lee's most sought after tales of sex and dismemberment.

"Trolley No. 1852" Edward Lee - In 1934, horror writer H.P. Lovecraft is invited to write a story for a subversive underground magazine, all on the condition that a pseudonym will be used. The pay is lofty, and God knows, Lovecraft needs the money. There's just one catch. It has to be a pornographic story . . . The 1852 Club is a bordello unlike any other. Its women are the most beautiful and they will do anything. But there is something else going on at this sex club. In the back rooms monsters are performing vile acts on each other and doors to other dimensions are opening . . .

"The Haunter of the Threshold" Edward Lee - There is something very wrong with this backwater town. Suicide notes, magic gems, and haunted cabins await her. Plus the woods are filled with monsters, both human and otherworldly. And then there are the horrible tentacles . . . Soon Hazel is thrown into a battle for her life that will test her sanity and sex drive. The sequel to H.P. Lovecraft's The Haunter of the Dark is Edward Lee's most pornographic novel to date!

"The Innswich Horror" Edward Lee - In July, 1939, antiquarian and H.P. Lovecraft aficionado, Foster Morley, takes a scenic bus tour through northern Massachusetts and finds Innswich Point. There far too many similarities between this fishing village and the fictional town of Love-craft's masterpiece, The Shadow Over Innsmouth. Join splatter king Edward Lee for a private tour of Innswich Point - a town founded on perversion, torture, and abominations from the sea.

"Highways to Hell" Bryan Smith - The road to hell is paved with angels and demons. Brain worms and dead prostitutes. Serial killers and frustrated writers. Zombies and Rock 'n Roll. And once you start down this path, there is no going back. Collecting thirteen tales of shock and terror from Bryan Smith, Highways to Hell is a non-stop road-trip of cruelty, pain, and death. Grab a seat, Smith has such sights to show you.

"Apeshit" Carlton Mellick III - Friday the 13th meets Visitor Q. Six hipster teens go to a cabin in the woods inhabited by a deformed killer. An incredibly fucked-up parody of B-horror movies with a bizarro slant

"The new gold standard in unstoppable fetus-fucking kill-freakomania . . . Genuine all-meat hardcore horror meets unadulterated Bizarro brainwarp strangeness. The results are beyond jaw-dropping, and fill me with pure, un-forgivable joy." - John Skipp

AVAILABLE FROM AMAZON.COM

deadite press

"Urban Gothic" Brian Keene - When their car broke down in a dangerous inner-city neighborhood, Kerri and her friends thought they would find shelter inside an old, dark row home. They thought they would be safe there until help arrived. They were wrong. The residents who live down in the cellar and the tunnels beneath the city are far more dangerous than the streets outside, and they have a very special way of dealing with trespassers. Trapped in a world of darkness, populated by obscene abominations, they will have to fight back if they ever want to see the sun again.

"Jack's Magic Beans" Brian Keene - It happens in a split-second. One moment, customers are happily shopping in the Save-A-Lot grocery store. The next instant, they are transformed into bloodthirsty psychotics, interested only in slaughtering one another and committing unimaginably atrocious and frenzied acts of violent depravity. Deadite Press is proud to bring one of Brian Keene's bleakest and most violent novellas back into print once more. This edition also includes four bonus short stories:

"Clickers" J. F. Gonzalez and Mark Williams- They are the Clickers, giant venomous blood-thirsty crabs from the depths of the sea. The only warning to their rampage of dismemberment and death is the terrible clicking of their claws. But these monsters aren't merely here to ravage and pillage. They are being driven onto land by fear. Something is hunting the Clickers. Something ancient and without mercy. *Clickers* is J. F. Gonzalez and Mark Williams' gore-soaked cult classic tribute to the giant monster B-movies of yesteryear.

"Clickers II" J. F. Gonzalez and Brian Keene- Thousands of Clickers swarm across the entire nation and march inland, slaughtering anyone and anything they come across. But this time the Clickers aren't blindly rushing onto land - they are being led by an intelligence older than civilization itself. A force that wants to take dry land away from the mammals. Those left alive soon realize that they must do everything and anything they can to protect humanity – no matter the cost. *This isn't war, this is extermination.*

"The Book of a Thousand Sins" Wrath James White - Welcome to a world of Zombie nymphomaniacs, psychopathic deities, voodoo surgery, and murderous priests. Where mutilation sex clubs are in vogue and torture machines are sex toys. No one makes it out alive – not even God himself.
"If Wrath James White doesn't make you cringe, you must be riding in the wrong end of a hearse."
   -Jack Ketchum

"Whargoul" Dave Brockie - It is a beast born in bullets and shrapnel, feeding off of pain, misery, and hard drugs. Cursed to wander the Earth without the hope of death, it is reborn again and again to spread the gospel of hate, abuse, and genocide. But what if it's not the only monster out there? What if there's something worse? From Dave Brockie, the twisted genius behind GWAR, comes a novel about the darkest days of the twentieth century.

"Take the Long Way Home" Brian Keene - All across the world, people suddenly vanish in the blink of an eye. Gone. Steve, Charlie and Frank were just trying to get home when it happened. Trapped in the ultimate traffic jam, they watch as civilization collapses, claiming the souls of those around them. God has called his faithful home, but the invitations for Steve, Charlie and Frank got lost. Now they must set off on foot through a nightmarish post-apocalyptic landscape in search of answers. In search of God. In search of their loved ones. And in search of home.

"Baby's First Book of Seriously Fucked-Up Shit" Robert Devereaux - From an orgy between God, Satan, Adam and Eve to beauty pageants for fetuses. From a giant human-absorbing tongue to a place where God is in the eyes of the psychopathic. This is a party at the furthest limits of human decency and cruelty. Robert Devereaux is your host but watch out, he's spiked the punch with drugs, sex, and dismemberment. Deadite Press is proud to present nine stories of the strange, the gross, and the just plain fucked up.

THE VERY BEST IN CULT HORROR

www.ingramcontent.com/pod-product-compliance
Lightning Source LLC
Chambersburg PA
CBHW060429260626
47161CB00005B/1846